P9-CFT-939

# Carlos Is Gonna Get It

# Carlos Is Gonna Get It

## KEVIN EMERSON

Arthur A. Levine Books

An Imprint of Scholastic Inc.

Text © 2008 by Kevin Emerson

Library of Congress Cataloging-in-Publication Data
Emerson, Kevin.
Carlos is gonna get it / by Kevin Emerson. — 1st ed.
p. cm.
Summary: Recounts the events that occur at the end of seventh grade, when a
group of friends plan to trick Carlos, an annoying "problem" student who says he is
visited by aliens, while they are on a field trip in the mountains of New Hampshire.
ISBN 978-0-439-93525-8 (hardcover : alk. paper) [1. Peer pressure—Fiction.
2. Practical jokes—Fiction. 3. Coming of age—Fiction. 4. Schools—Fiction.
5. African Americans—Fiction. 6. Boston (Mass.)—Fiction. 7. New Hampshire—
Fiction.] I. Title
PZ7. E5853Car 2008
[Fic] -dc22          2007037088

ISBN-13: 978-0-439-93525-8
ISBN-10: 0-439-93525-3
10 9 8 7 6 5 4 3 2 1      08 09 10 11 12

Book design by Becky Terhune

First edition, October 2008

Printed in the U.S.A. 23

*For the students and teachers at NHCS . . .*

# Carlos Is Gonna Get It

# CHAPTER 1
# Yet Another "Day After"

**W**e decided to play a trick on Carlos. 'Cause Carlos, he had problems. Lots of 'em. Sometimes he was just too annoying, and by the end of seventh grade, we just couldn't take it anymore.

Now, Carlos had always been strange. No matter where you were or what you were doing, you could always count on him to be having some kind of problem. Back in sixth grade, my best friend, Sara, and I even made this list of his most common ones:

PROBLEMS THAT CARLOS HAS:

1. He's too small all the time.

2. Almost every day he finds a way to trip and fall on his face without anyone's help.

3. He always steals things, but, like, the same things, over and over.

4. Right in the middle of class he'll pull up his shirt and start scratching himself and you know that's REALLY GROSS.

5. If you end up in a study group with him, like we always do, all he wants to study is aliens.

Then in seventh grade, Carlos started having these days where he would act so crazy and annoying that you would just about want to die. We called a day like that a "Day After," and they happened about once a month. We figured they would just stop after a while, but they didn't, and the one that happened at the end of May was the last straw.

We were in social studies class, first period Monday. Ms. Atkinson was going on and on about the causes of World War II, but whatever. She might as well have been relaxing on the couch at home for how much we were paying attention to her, because Carlos was late, so we were all on high alert.

I was sitting next to Sara, like I always did, and every minute we were glancing up at the clock, then

2

at the door, then at each other to raise our eyebrows, and then around the room to raise our eyebrows at our friends Thea, Donte, and Frankie. You might think we'd be laughing about our little routine, but we were dead serious, because with every minute that Carlos didn't show up, we felt more and more sure that a Day After was on the way.

Normally, Carlos was the first kid at school in the morning. His mom worked nights for the police and dropped him off before she went to bed for the day. It was like, no matter how early you got to school, there was Carlos, sitting with his tiny elbows on his tiny knees, and his big head in his tiny hands. I knew because twice a week I came to school early for book club with Ms. Stanton, who always showed up late. I'd end up waiting around, and there would be Carlos, and so we'd end up talking, whether I wanted to or not, until the first bus arrived. And so if Carlos wasn't on those steps in the morning — that was the first sign of trouble.

Now the minutes ticked by slower than ever. We kept watching the classroom door for the second sign of a Day After: the Hair. And sure enough, halfway through class, we saw it.

It appeared at the door before the rest of his head,

a huge tower of frizz picked straight up and off to the left. Sara gasped when she saw it. I rolled my eyes and turned to find Thea, Donte, and Frankie, who were doing the same. Then there was Carlos, standing in the doorway, looking like he didn't even know where he was.

"Well, good morning, Carlos," Ms. Atkinson said, like she was suddenly really tired. She knew the signs too and knew it was going to be a long day. "Nice of you to join us," she said, but I wondered if she meant it. I mean, you knew she cared about him — you could tell that Ms. Atkinson cared about all of us, even when we were being major pains — but still, sometimes you could also tell that, like, everything was too much for her. Now when I tell you that she was in her late twenties you might think that's all gross and old, but you know it's not for teachers. Most of the teachers in our school were, like, young. You weren't going to find those old and mean teachers coming to Dorchester to teach a bunch of city kids. Sometimes when the class would be having one of our crazy times, where things just got out of control, I would look at Ms. Atkinson and think: *God, why would you want to be a teacher and do this to yourself?* — especially when Carlos was acting like he did.

4

Anyway, the third sign that you were smack-dab in the middle of a Day After was when Carlos answered in *that voice*.

"Go-od mo-or-ning-g," Carlos said, sounding like he was being shaken really fast.

"Problems!" Donte suddenly shouted from the back of the room, like he always did. Everybody cracked up.

"Tweedo!" Frankie joined in, like he always did, but only Donte laughed. That was their little joke. It was because of this little robot at the science museum. We went on a field trip back in fifth grade and there was this exhibit called House of the Future, and Tweedo was this little gold robot who was just a cartoon that would explain different features of the house to you. You would press a button next to, like, the solar toaster or whatever, and Tweedo would appear on a TV screen to tell you how it worked.

"That's enough!" Ms. Atkinson snapped, giving both Frankie and Donte a check next to their names in the corner of the blackboard. "Donte, Frankie," Ms. Atkinson went on, all serious and no fun now, "you know that calling out is unacceptable, as is making fun of your peers —" And here was something

5

that really annoyed us all about Carlos's Day Afters: Everybody always got in more trouble because of them.

Donte grumbled, "We weren't making fun of —"

But Ms. Atkinson wasn't hearing it. "If that kind of behavior continues, you'll both be sent to Principal Davis, is that clear?"

Meanwhile, Carlos slowly shuffled to his seat. His white button-down shirt was all sloppy and untucked, his sneakers were untied, and his two-sizes-too-big khaki pants were all grass-stained at the knees and barely held up by a brown belt cinched all the way to the last hole.

He walked past Sara and me, his head bent off to the left like he was fighting an invisible magnet in the sky. He looked at me and for a second I freaked because I thought he might break our early-morning rule: Talking on the front steps when no one else was around was fine, but talking during school was not allowed. Luckily, even though he opened his mouth a little, he didn't say hello. He just headed for his seat at a table in the back, where he sat down and started twitching. I breathed a sigh of relief, but I also felt my stomach drop. One of the worst parts about these

Day Afters was that despite how annoying they were, I kind of felt bad for Carlos, which you know I could never tell my friends.

So poor Ms. Atkinson finished her lecture to Donte and Frankie, then tried to keep teaching us. She started on again about the war. By the way, how annoying was it that there was only a month more of school, and we had, like, sixty years of history left before we got to the present day? What's the point of learning history if you're not going to get to the present day? It's like playing a board game and stopping before anybody wins.

Ms. Atkinson was lecturing from the other side of her big desk and so she couldn't hear it but, like, all of us were counting to ourselves. You could hear this soft lip-clicking as we counted down to the fourth sign of a Day After. And sure enough, three minutes and twenty-seven seconds after Carlos had walked into the room, Sara and I looked nervously over our shoulders, still whispering —

"Two . . . one . . ."

"O-oh n-o —" Carlos moaned, and *bang!* He fell right out of his chair, landing mostly on the floor but partly on Frankie.

"Ow! What's with you, Tweedo?!" Frankie shouted, like he always did when Carlos fell on him.

Donte snorted. "Problems . . ." He started laughing all showy into his elbow.

"Frankie!" Ms. Atkinson was spinning around from the board. "Donte! That's it! Two checks and go to Principal Davis's office, now!"

The room hushed.

"God, that's so unfair, man!" Donte huffed as he shoved back from his desk and stood up.

"Make it three checks," Ms. Atkinson said icily.

Someone snickered quietly from the corner, and Donte and Frankie walked out of the room with their heads all hanging low like sad dogs.

"So-or-ry," Carlos squeaked as he slowly crawled back into his chair.

"Carlos," Ms. Atkinson said once the boys were gone, "do you need a minute?"

Giving Carlos a minute outside was one of the things that all the teachers did with him on Day Afters. None of the rest of us got to leave class without being in trouble. See if any of us could fall out of our chairs in the middle of class without getting at least a check by our name! But we all knew Carlos was on a Special Plan. Dr. Johnson, the school psychologist who sat with him during math class — and whose office you would see Carlos in, like, all the time — and the Therapy Lady who came and took him during music, they always brought this thick orange folder with Carlos's name on it.

"No-o, tha-nks," Carlos groaned.

But we all knew better. And half an hour later, we started counting down again, and right on cue — *bang*, Carlos fell out of his chair again, this time off the other side and right onto Maurice, a big kid who got in trouble like he was a magnet for it.

"Get off me, runt!" Maurice scowled. That was good for three checks for Maurice, who had more than almost everyone else in the class combined, and a trip to Principal Davis too.

"Carlos," Ms. Atkinson said, looking like she was about to just give up and walk out, "I want you to go to Dr. Johnson's office now."

"*O-o-kay.*"

Now you might think that was the last we would see of Carlos, but no. Carlos was back for math, and even though he was sitting with Dr. Johnson, we were all just waiting for the fifth and final phase of a Day After to begin: the scratching.

By now, you may be wondering why we called these

9

days with Carlos Day Afters. Well, it was because on one of those mornings, when we were both early and waiting out on the front steps, I asked him:

"Carlos, why do you have those days when you have, like, extra problems?"

He looked up at me like he was thinking hard, then answered with a totally serious face: "Well," he said in his tiny voice, "those are the days after I get the visits."

"What visits?" I asked.

He leaned close to me and put a hand to his mouth. "The visits from *them*."

"Them who?"

"You know . . ." He looked out across the parking lot to make sure we were alone, then he said it: "Aliens."

I just stared, waiting for him to laugh or something, but he looked away and started scratching his bony ankles through his socks. You know I wished I'd never even asked.

So on the way to math, Thea had passed by Sara and me on the stairs and said: "Hey, Trina, your soda says he'll be scratching by the end of math."

"Yours says he won't start until art," I replied.

Thea was always making bets with Frankie, Donte, Sara, and me. It was fun, but honestly, it was like giving away your lunch, that's how good Thea was at betting. She had an eye for predicting what would happen, which was why she was the best of the five of us at making plans for playing tricks on people.

Thea was so good at betting that Ms. Atkinson had made it a rule that Thea couldn't be seen with anyone else's food during lunch. So of course, if you lost a bet with Thea, you had to sit there and not eat your yummy treats, saving them to give to her after school.

And with only ten minutes to go in math class, I suddenly knew that I would spend lunch staring longingly at my grape soda without getting to drink it. We had just started a quiz, and everybody was being quiet, so we all heard the fifth phase of the Day After begin:

*Ruffle-ruffle* . . . First the rubbing on the outside of the shirt, over his stomach.

*Ruffle-ruffle* . . . *Swish — shuffle — scratchscratch-scratch* — Then the shirt coming all untucked — I looked back, and it was horrible. There was little Carlos, slouched in his chair, with his shirt all up to

11

his neck and both hands scratching his bony belly like he was trying to claw the skin right off. Dr. Johnson was saying something quietly to him, but whatever it was, it wasn't helping.

*"Sh-sh-sh!"* Caitlin hissed from across the aisle.

*Scratchscratchscratch* —

"Carlos," I heard Dr. Johnson say more loudly, "focus on your work."

"Carlos," Ms. Williams said, "do you need to hear that problem again?"

"That's o-kay, Ms. Dou-ble-you" — *scratchscratch-SCRATCH* — "I'm all right."

"No you ain't! You got problems!" Thea shouted, always at her worst in math to impress Raheem, the fine eighth-grade boy who had to come to the seventh-grade class.

"Thea!" Now it was Ms. Williams's turn to lose her temper, like she always did. And it was like: *Here we go again.* Next thing you knew, Thea was in trouble and Dr. Johnson was leading still-scratching Carlos out the door.

Now, you might think that we would've been happy about *that* part of the Day Afters — I mean the distraction and the getting nothing done, but honestly, can you really imagine having this happen all the time? Being with the same twenty kids totally gets on your nerves by the end of May no matter what, and having Carlos's craziness too . . . Ugh.

And so our day went on and on like it was the longest ever — not just because of Carlos but also because I couldn't wait to get to our secret after-school meeting place, the Tubs. See, at lunch, Thea had passed by Sara and me and leaned over:

"He is so annoying," she said under her breath. "I can't take it anymore."

We all gazed across the room, to where Carlos had peeled apart his sandwich and was rubbing the mustard from the bread onto his arm.

"Oh my God, I know," I muttered. What I also thought was annoying was that I was feeling bad for him again, but of course I wasn't going to say anything about that.

"Well, girls, don't worry," Thea whispered, leaning even closer. "I have a plan to get Carlos good."

# CHAPTER 2
# The Tubs and Thea's Plan

So that afternoon we all met at the Tubs to hang out, like we always did after school. Sara and I were late, 'cause we had a writing group, and so we rushed to get there. If Thea had a plan, we didn't want to miss a second of it.

Thea loved to make plans. Even for something as simple as tripping somebody on the way down the stairs to art class. Her plans were always complicated and intriguing, and she always had a role for everyone involved. Even though Sara and I knew that they were kinda wrong, because they always involved somebody either getting embarrassed or a little hurt, we liked being part of them, and what can I say? Don't you know how sometimes it feels good to be bad, especially if you're good, like, most of the time?

We had a list for this too:

## REASONS WHY WE LIKE BEING A PART OF THEA'S EVIL PLANS:

1. You get to be in on a secret.

2. Even if by the time the plan goes into action, everybody, even the person who the plan is against, knows about it, which always happens, you still knew about it *first*.

3. Thea will always back you up when you have to prove that you knew about it first, unless she's mad at you for something, so you always stay on her good side.

4. Even though you're part of the plan, you only ever have to play a small part, and Thea is good about never getting you in trouble 'cause she knows she'll need you in on her next one.

5. Sometimes, you just need to let loose. All these other kids are

doing things wrong all the time.
It's not fair!

And it's not like Thea's plans were *really* mean or anything. Most of them were just the usual — like tripping one kid because he called another kid ugly. In a way, we were like the school police force. Sure, the person who got tripped would be mad and hollering and pouting during recess and all, but an hour later everyone would be over it and have moved on to the next big drama.

Thea liked to be cool, but more than that, she just liked to be in charge of something. I think she started making plans because she wanted to impress India, Latoya, and Kim Chi. Those three girls were definitely considered the coolest in our grade, and always acted like they were all old and everything. Thea wanted to hang with them, but they weren't really interested in her, probably because her plans weren't nasty enough. Plus, India, Latoya, and Kim Chi are kind of fashionable and always like to look good, and not that Thea doesn't look fine and all, but she's kind of a big girl and sometimes she gets a hard time about that.

The other problem for Thea is that she's kinda

smart and does well in school. She can't help herself, she just is. So when those girls weren't interested in her, she made her own little group with us smarter-but-lesser-troublemakers.

Anyway, by the time Sara and I got to the Tubs, all the snack bags that Frankie and Donte had pocketed from the school kitchen were lying in the grass like popped balloons. Everybody was in their bathtub laughing with their elbows and knees hooked over the sides. There were, like, a hundred bathtubs in the high grass behind this rusty old warehouse, but we had put five in a circle like flower petals. The field of bathtubs was right beside the train tracks, and Highway 93 roared beyond that. As Sara and I came around the corner, we heard everybody *still* recovering from the Day After:

"I know, man." Frankie — whining like he always did. "And finally Mr. Fissile was, like, '*Carlos, what are you doing?*' and he turned around and he was all embarrassed 'cause he had the — the thing —"

"It's called a magnifying glass." Thea — correcting Frankie like she always did.

"Euh, it's a magnifying glass!" Donte — mocking Thea like he always did.

"Yeah, so, like, Carlos had the magnifier glass, the thing, whatever." Frankie — getting annoyed because he didn't always know the words for things. "And then he said: *'But Mr. Fissile, I'm just itchy is all!'* And he was all scratching himself with the magnifier under his shirt!"

We all groaned together.

"Ugh, he is so gross!" Thea shivered, but you could only see her feet and hands wiggling over the edge of her tub, which was the deepest one, so deep that she had to sit on her backpack just to rest her head on the back edge.

Sara and I hopped into our tubs. You know, I guess it sounds kinda strange for a bunch of kids to be hanging out in old empty bathtubs, but if you'd been there, you would get that it's the best. Here's our list of what it's like:

### WHAT THE TUBS IS LIKE:

1. It's a secret place, so I'm not going to tell you exactly how to get there or make a map or anything.

2. Nobody knows about the Tubs except for the five of us.

3. The five of us are: Sara, Frankie, Donte, Thea, and me — Trina.

4. Okay, there are a few other kids who know about it, but they would never show up there, 'cause they *KNOW what would happen.*

5. The Tubs is the only place to go where nobody hassles you, except of course for your friends, which is sometimes worse than anybody else.

It was Thea who first learned about the Tubs. Her older sister showed her. She said you wouldn't want to be going there at night, but after school it would be fine. Thea told India, Latoya, and Kim Chi about it, back when she was trying to make plans with them, but they acted too old and cool to hang out in a bunch of bathtubs. So Thea showed the Tubs to Sara and me. The three of us have been in the same reading groups and math groups and all since I swear, like, second grade, when the school opened. She would be in the after-school clubs with us too, if her attitude didn't get her in trouble.

Now Donte made a face like he just bit into that orange stuff they call chicken in the school lunches. "What's his problem anyway?" Donte always had that scowl on his face. He was big enough to look like he belonged in seventh grade with us, but he still had those kind of baby-fat cheeks. He had on his black Raiders hat and his black sneakers that were nicer than he needed but that's how his mom spoiled him.

"Who?" Frankie asked. He was taller and kind of a beanpole, with his pants a couple inches too short because he only had, like, two pairs and I swear he grew, like, an inch a week.

"Duh, wake up, idiot!" Thea — rolling her eyes. She shook her hands and when she did her tangles of bracelets jingled. She had her hair straightened and with a streak of red, and it curled under right at her shoulders. "Carlos! That's who we've, like, been talking about!"

"Euh, you're an idiot!" Donte — shaking his head at Thea.

"Oh my God, you guys, shut up!" I finally shouted. And you may be wondering why oh why three smart and clever girls would ever ever ever show a secret special place like the Tubs to a couple of boys, especially Donte and Frankie. We even wondered ourselves sometimes. Well, see, it wasn't just because my parents and Donte's mom have been friends basically forever — there's even pictures from when we were little, of us dressed up and standing together like we *like* each other, which you need to know has never been the case.

And it wasn't just because Donte and Frankie overheard us talking about the Tubs one time last spring and then secretly followed us all the way there, 'cause if we had told them not to ever come back, they wouldn't have, because they would've *known what would happen* if they did.

Really, I think it was because, well, it's kind of fun to have boys around. Sure, they're all annoying and immature and get on your nerves, but it's fun to hear their dumb jokes, and it's fun to run circles around their silly minds — and it's even fun to get into fights with them.

Oh, and also, Sara and I knew there'd always been some secret *liking* going on between Donte and Thea, like more than either of them would ever admit.

"All I'm sayin'," Thea muttered, "is that Carlos has too many problems and it's getting on my nerves too much. I can't even concentrate in class."

"You mean concentrate on Raheem!" Donte — never missing a chance to bring that up.

"*Ohhh!*" Frankie shouted, pumping his fist in the air like he always did.

And it's hard to imagine Thea jumping clear out of her huge tub, but you know she did because if there was one thing that she never took, it was Donte, the boy she secretly liked, making fun of her about Raheem, the boy she pretended to like. Sara looked at me and we did our eye-rolling thing together.

After Thea made sure to give Frankie a punch too, she climbed back into her tub. "Well then," she continued like nothing had happened, except that she was out of breath. She's not exactly into sports. "Now that we're all here . . ."

This was Thea setting the stage for her latest plan, and we all knew it. We all sat up in our tubs, except for Sara, who put her head down.

"It's time we talked about that little weirdo and his problems," Thea said like she was suddenly a wise old professor. "Y'all think he's as annoying as I do, right?"

Me: "*Mmmm-hmm.*"

Frankie: "*Tsssss!*"

Donte: "*Tchyuh!*"

"Well, just think —" Thea continued, "how bad he's going to be on *the trip*."

"Oh man," Donte muttered.

The trip was four weeks away. Ms. Atkinson was taking the seventh grade on a two-day trip to the White Mountains in New Hampshire. That meant hiking and compasses and waterfalls, but what it meant most of all was:

Overnight. Sara and I didn't even have to make a list of the most fun things that you could ever do at school, because *overnight* was so number one that nothing else could even sit in the other four spots.

"Let's just remember, shall we," Thea said, "exactly what's at stake on the overnight. Trina?"

"Of course," I answered, pushing my blue-beaded braids off my shoulders like I was the chief record-keeper. "I believe we have a list for that. Sara?"

"Hmm?" Sara looked up and her white face got all pink. Nobody else knew why, but I did. Sara had been secretly reading. She always sat there, with her sandy-brown hair falling over her face, and everyone else thinking she was just nodding off, because we all knew that Sara got up at, like, five every morning and went to swim practice — but really she was reading.

Sara pulled the same reading trick during school, with a book in her lap under her desk. I think the teachers knew, but they also knew that she was a big-time swimmer, and she got all A's anyway. This was how she always got all her schoolwork done and still had time to read her crazy books, but more about them later.

I gave Sara a second to hide her book, then asked her again. "List of the best things about an overnight?"

"Oh yeah! Just a sec . . ." She reached down by her feet and dug around in her backpack.

"God, Sara." Donte — snickering. "What, did you pack for a week in Florida or something?" He glanced over at Frankie, all proud of his joke, but then I cleared my throat.

And I was like: "Shut up, Donte, just because you never bring home any books and your bag is all empty — why you need a bag with wheels when all you bring home is your wrestling magazine. That's all I'm sayin'."

"Whatever." Donte looked sideways at me, waving his hand like he wasn't listening. What's annoying about Donte is that he is kind of smart but just doesn't try.

24

"Here it is," Sara said, holding up a piece of my yellow paper with the purple lines, the only kind we used for making lists. "Ahem . . ." She pretended like she was clearing her throat and smiled, 'cause she was one of those people who seemed to get even more comfortable when the spotlight was on her:

"COOLEST THINGS ABOUT
GOING ON AN OVERNIGHT:
1. Flashlights
2. Pajamas
3. Whispering
4. Secrets
5. Sneaking out."

"That's it?" Thea asked, trying to sit up higher in her deep tub but then sliding back down anyway. "That's your whole list? There's way more than th — what?"

She said *what* because Sara and I did that thing where we smiled at each other and rolled our eyes like we knew everything, or at least something that Thea didn't. Thea couldn't stand that. She had her plans and her bets, but Sara and I had our secret facts and faces, which helped even things out.

"*What?!*"

"Thea," I said, like I was a big know-it-all, "no good list can have more than five things on it, otherwise it gets boring. Five is the most reasons you can have for why something is the way it is before it just seems like there's too many reasons, and maybe there's something wrong."

"Whatever." Thea — annoyed whenever she didn't know stuff. "Anyway," she went on, pulling the spotlight back to her, "so the overnight is coming up, and everyone's still going, right?"

We all nodded. So far, none of us had the ten checks next to our name in that corner of Ms. Atkinson's chalkboard. We were all at less than seven checks with only four weeks to go, and only one person in the whole class had more than six. That was Maurice. He had seventeen.

"And you know Carlos is going to be there, no matter what," Thea said.

"That's because you know he's never gonna get ten checks." Frankie — whining again.

"That's because *he* never gets checks when he gets in trouble," Donte said. "It's not fair."

"No, he doesn't get checks most of the time because you two and Maurice always *get* him in trouble." Thea — shaking her head at Donte. "And all the teachers know it. But all the other times, like today with his Day After, he doesn't get any checks because he's on a Special Plan."

"And the teachers try to keep him included in class." Sara — not looking up from her book.

"I hate that!" Frankie moaned.

"Dork!" Donte — pointing at Frankie. "You're on a Special Plan too!"

"So? I keep my problems to myself. I ain't all annoying like him!"

"Face it," Thea continued, "there's no way to keep Carlos from going on the trip. And the teachers will want him there because he never gets to go anywhere 'cause his mom works, like, all the time. So he'll all be there and, knowing him, he'll freak out and ruin it for everyone. Ms. Atkinson will have to sit up with him all night and so none of us will be able to sneak out or nothing."

"He's totally going to do something like that!" I agreed. "Just like fifth grade, on the science museum overnight . . . and that was before these Day Afters."

We all groaned, even Sara, who was still reading.

"God!" Frankie — punching the side of his tub. "I hate that kid, man!"

"So, I've been thinking . . ." Thea put a finger to the side of her chin like she was thinking really hard. "We can't stop Carlos from going . . . and it's obvious he's going to have his *alien* problems. . . ." She was playing it up now. "And there's no way we can stop that, unless . . ."

"Unless what?" All of us — desperate to know what Thea was scheming, letting her be the drama queen. Even Sara was looking up again and actually had her secret book on the edge of her tub, but nobody even noticed.

"Unless . . ." Thea — up on her knees now, a gleam in her eye. "He really *was* visited by aliens." She put her hands out and started nodding slowly.

"Ooohh . . ." We all nodded slowly too, and then leaned back, letting the words sink in.

Now we all felt the usual vibrations in our tubs, meaning that the T was going to pass by. The Red Line subway came out from underground just a little ways north of the Tubs and passed right by us, ten feet off the ground, on the other side of a tall chain-link fence with barbed wire at the top. The big silver snake slithered by, shuddering from side to side, sparks jumping out from where it touched the electrified third rail. I liked to watch the faces crowded together inside, heading down to Ashmont to find their way home from another day. I always wondered if any of them ever noticed us. I mean, even if you were looking out the window, would you be looking for five kids sitting in a mess of old bathtubs?

It was a good thing that the train passed by right then, because we all needed a minute to really get what the heck Thea was talking about. You *know* Frankie and Donte didn't get it, but they would just act like they did until they figured it out. I was close. I mean, I got what she was saying: If Carlos was always using this excuse about aliens to be all weird and get attention, then naturally a *real* alien visit would maybe scare him into stopping. Of course, I was pretty sure that Thea didn't have any idea how to summon real aliens.

The train was almost past us now, the rumble fading away.

"So the aliens will have to look real," I said.

"So that Carlos is convinced." Sara — picking it up.

"Like costumes, but not all homemade."

"And when we scare Carlos with *real* aliens..."
Thea — nodding. "It'll teach him to stop pretending about his problems."

I looked over at Sara, who was looking over at me with that little smile that played on the left corner of her mouth, the secret one that no parents or schoolteachers or annoying boys ever got to see. It was sinister, devious, and so much fun!

"Yeeaahh." I grinned, nodding.

Thea was smiling like she had pizza for lunch. "*Mmm-hmm*... Now, of course we can't do it *before* the trip, because then we might not get to go. Besides, when does Carlos say that he's getting visited by these aliens? At night... So we'll have to make *our* visit at night too. And —" Now Thea rose to her feet, like the ringmaster getting our total attention for the finale. "When are we going to be all together at night?"

"On the trip thing!" Frankie — grinning all proud, even if he *still* didn't really get it.

"He's going to do something mental anyway," Sara added, now seeing how brilliant it was. "So why wait for it to happen?"

"Exactly." Thea — nodding. "Why let him have all his problems and ruin it for the rest of us like he always does? Let's plan on it instead."

You had to hand it to Thea. These kinds of ideas, and the guts to really pull them off, were worth all of her attitude, and believe me, she had a lot of it.

"On our trip to New Hampshire," Thea concluded, "Carlos is going to get more than he bargained for, when he gets an alien visit from *us*."

"Yeah!" Donte — finally getting it, and Sara and I and Thea laughed.

"What's so funny?" Frankie asked, and we laughed even harder.

Boys.

We left the Tubs that afternoon with assignments:

### THINGS TO DO FOR THE TRICK:

1. Sara: Research aliens and alien sightings.

2. Me: Help Sara and think of what we'll need.

3. Thea: Plan out the parts of the trick.

4. Donte: Try to keep his mouth shut (that should be enough).

5. Frankie: Help Donte keep his mouth shut.

As we walked back around the warehouse, making our way along a narrow dirt path bordering a brick sound wall next to the T tracks and Highway 93, we all practiced talking in monotone alien voices.

"I am Tweedus, your father," Donte said.

"Tweedo, you will come in our spaceship," Sara even added.

Everyone was into it except me. I was just walking along with a safe smile, listening.

Because there was one problem. It wasn't that this plan was more risky and complicated than usual. And it wasn't that Carlos didn't deserve it, because didn't he, for being so annoying all the time, and never controlling himself, and never getting in trouble for it?

The only problem with playing a trick on Carlos was that I didn't really want to, but I knew that I had to.

# CHAPTER 3
# Two Tragedies Before
# Eight O'Clock

**W**e didn't talk much about the trick for the rest of that week, and then a whole weekend went by, so by the time I woke up the next Monday morning, I was feeling pretty relieved. It almost seemed like all that talk about the trick was just a dream. Still, I knew better. Once Thea got her mind on a plan, she wouldn't stop until it happened.

So why didn't I want to do the trick? I blame my parents. It's their fault for raising me with a little guilt-demon living in my stomach. I can't ever just do something without having to worry about whether it's *right*. Now, don't worry, I can usually overcome it, especially when it comes to normal things, like a plan to trip Shawn because he calls Caitlin fat. I mean, Caitlin gets revenge, Shawn falls on his face, and like I said, an hour later everyone's moved on to the next drama anyway.

But that was the problem with playing this trick on Carlos. He wasn't normal. And while most kids just figured he made his problems up to get attention, I wasn't so sure. I had to be stuck wondering about Carlos's *feelings*. I had to feel bad for him for having problems. Because, like, if he was only doing this whole Day After thing to get attention, then why did he seem so miserable about it all the time? And that made me feel like I *shouldn't* be annoyed by him, even when I was. Stupid guilt-demon!

Thea was right — Carlos was going to end up ruining the overnight. And I wasn't going to let down my friends. I mean, what would I say to them? *Hey, guys, I feel too guilty to do the trick because I'm worried about Carlos's feelings?* Yeah, right! See me live *that* one down anytime soon!

So I woke up Monday morning still wondering what I was going to do about it all, not knowing that by the time first period started, things would be a whole lot worse.

I got up on time, every part of me snapping awake, and there was a special feeling in the air — the first day of June. When all the days start to smooth over, and it's like, before you were walking down a staircase toward summer, now you're sliding, and it's so thrilling but sad too, because you really want to hang on to every moment, but the slide is so fast that the tears are getting grabbed by the wind and torn off your face — or something like that is what June always feels like. I love it. I wait all year for it. Then it comes and I can't keep up.

Sara and I had talked about it on Friday. Sara's June feeling is different, because the summer is all about important things for her. I swear she never stops getting up early and going to practice at this pool club down in Milton: the Pines. And she has to be there at, like, five because the Dorchester team is just renting use of the pool. She'll do that until the end of July and then it's off to swim camp out in Arizona, which is, like, where the Junior Olympics kids train. Sara is really so unbelievably good at swimming you can hardly believe it. But maybe you can imagine that it's a lot, especially compared to me, who does, like, nothing except go to overnight camp for a couple weeks in August. Sometimes you can see it on her face.

Sara's first swim meet of the summer season had happened on Sunday. I couldn't wait to talk to her about it on the way to school.

So I was up and dressed, smelling the sweet air, the way it gets when the day is going to be so smoking hot by ten. I washed my face and tied my new braids with nice long extensions back in one neat ponytail.

In the kitchen, I found Dad sitting at the little table by the front window, the one that lets him read the paper and look down at the people walking by on the street. Our apartment is on the second floor of a big old house that's owned by my grandma Rae, who lives downstairs. She's Dad's mom.

Dad gets up early, like, every day even when he doesn't have to, and I swear, what is up with that? Mom is almost the same way, but not *so* much. The only thing I can figure is that when you get older, you don't need to sleep as much, because there's not as much interesting stuff going on in your life.

"Hey there," Dad said, all twice as bright and chipper as anyone should be in the morning.

"Hi." Me — still grumbly, grabbing my absolute favorite cereal bowl, the one with the picture of my favorite diva, Heavyn, inside at the bottom. I'm not even going to get into talking about Heavyn right now, but let me just say that when you find her smiling back at you from the bottom of your cereal bowl, you feel like you could do anything.

"Did you get all your homework done?" Dad asked as he leafed through the paper.

"Of course." I poured a bowl of cereal and sat down across from him.

"You did? Well now —" he scrunched his brow — "what I'm wondering is, was that while you were watching the Fright Night Triple Feature, or maybe while you were snoring the Sunday afternoon away —"

"I don't snore! You're the one who snores!"

"And you know you have my nose, honey — wait, I got it. Maybe it was while you were taking that half-hour shower after dinner last night. That's it, right?"

By the way, this is how me and my dad talk most of the time. It's a lucky thing and don't I know it. I mean, I have him right where I want him, you know? I am the envy of all for that.

So, I was scooping milky spoonfuls of Magic Mouthwatering Miniature Marshmallow Monsters (that's a long name, I know, but I just call them MMMMM's . . . like the sound of how good they are), when Dad said:

"We have to leave a little early today."

"Ahh knoo," I said between chomping mouthfuls of cereal, "booggroup."

"Earlier than that," Dad said. "Sara's mom called. Sara hurt her leg at the swim meet yesterday, and now she's on crutches. She'll need extra time."

I couldn't believe it. When we got to Sara's house, she was down on the sidewalk, leaning on crutches, with her right ankle wrapped in a bright orange cast. Her mom stood beside her holding her backpack.

"Oh my God, Sara, are you okay?" I jumped out and grabbed her bag.

"It could be worse," Sara said like she didn't really think so.

"What happened?"

"I slipped on the pool deck," she said, looking away, "while I was running out of the bathroom for a race."

I thought about what I should say next, then immediately said what I shouldn't: "Does this mean you won't be able to go on the overnight?"

"Sara has a few more worries right now than a school trip," Sara's mom said, handing her backpack to me. She was dressed all nice in a tan suit, and she looked annoyed. "Now, Sara, remember, your ankle comes first. No recess — not even sharpening a pencil without your crutches. You have to stay completely off it so that it will heal."

"I know, Mom." Sara — grumbling like she'd already heard this a hundred times.

As soon as we were in the car, I got down to business trying to cheer her up. "Okay, now you're going to need a personal assistant," I said, turning to her and pulling my math homework out of my bag. "I went ahead and made a list on the way over. Want to hear it?"

"All right," Sara said, but she just looked away.

"Does your leg hurt?"

"It hasn't stopped hurting," she muttered.

"Okay." I held up the list. "Well, I'm here to make it better. Here we go:

"IMPORTANT THINGS THAT THE PERSONAL ASSISTANT TO SARA MUST DO:

1. Clear the way of kids who are too stupid to notice that the girl with crutches is coming and obviously needs some space.

39

2. Carry her backpack.

3. Deliver all punches to all boys who deserve them on her behalf.

4. Copy all homework assignments and do all homework during other classes, except science, which may be worth paying attention to.

5. Use secret dirt that we have on ALL the boys in the class to get them to wait on Sara's every need."

I looked at Sara, proud of my list, but she just kept staring out the window. "Sounds great," she said, like she didn't think so.

"I'm sorry." Me — not really knowing what else to say.

"Yeah, whatever," Sara muttered.

"Accidents happen."

But that just made Sara's face get redder. "My dad doesn't think so. He says if I hadn't been stalling in the bathroom, I wouldn't have had to rush. Now they don't want me to go on the trip."

"That's no fair!"

"It depends on my next doctor's appointment."

We drove the rest of the way with the car all strangely quiet. Dad dropped us off, and we were nice and early, so of course, who did we have to find on the steps of school? You guessed it.

"Hi, Trina. Hi, Sara." There was Carlos, with his chin in his hands, elbows on his knees. He looked normal today, his hair back in cornrows, his shirt actually tucked in.

"Hi, Carlos."

"Sorry about last week," he said, "and my Day After." Here's the thing about Carlos's voice: Even on a normal day, it was way higher than a seventh grader's should be, but what was worse was that it sounded like he had a stuffy nose all the time. And actually, he wiped his nose just then. Some kids get sick a lot. I thought for a second how it would be too bad for Carlos if he had all those other problems and on top of that he was sick all the time.

I dropped our bags to the steps. "Uh-huh."

Now he finally noticed Sara's ankle. "What happened?" Whenever Carlos asked a question, his voice got especially squeaky.

"She broke her ankle," I snapped. "Duh, what does it look like?"

Carlos put his chin back in his hands. "Sorry."

Now see, this is exactly what I'm talking about. Standing there, I suddenly felt this horrible knot of guilt start to burn in my belly, and just like every other time, I ended up talking to Carlos again. I was like: "So . . . your mom worked late again?"

Carlos looked up, like he always did, like he was surprised I was talking to him. "She always does."

"Hmm. It must suck to get here so early every day."

"Oh, I don't mind really." Now he lifted his head and looked toward the leafy trees at the edge of the parking lot. "Sometimes I see raccoons!" Then he sighed. "But not lately."

"Um, yeah." I looked over to Sara, planning on us rolling our eyes at Carlos's weirdness, but she was just staring off into space. I turned back to Carlos. One interesting thing about him was that his mom sometimes saw cool stuff in her police job. "So," I asked him, "has your mom seen any more violence lately?"

"Well . . ." Carlos had his chin back in his hands. "Lately she's just been writing parking tickets and stuff, but oh —" His face lit up again. "The other night there was this guy who called" — Carlos suddenly jumped to his feet — "and he was totally crazy

42

because his girl was coming after him with a knife, right? And —"

"Whoa." I held my hands out. "Okay, Carlos, let's not get too crazy."

"Oh, okay. Roger." He sat back down.

Thankfully, the first bus rolled in a minute later, and we were done talking.

Just before social studies started, our science teacher, Mr. Fissile, suddenly popped his head in. I figured he was here to get in his morning flirting with Ms. Atkinson, because we all knew those two were all gross and in love, even if they denied it. But instead, he stepped in front of the class.

"Morning, everyone," he said, holding a sinister index card in his hand. "I heard Ms. Atkinson was going to be giving you some more details about your trip this morning, so I thought I'd announce the pairings for your end-of-the-year science projects."

We all groaned. Donte sucked his teeth.

"I'm telling you now," Mr. Fissile continued, "because you'll be required to complete your project on time and successfully in order to go on the trip with us."

Quieter but even more annoyed groaning now. Teachers and their traps!

So, like, you would think that was the worst of it, but no no no. Mr. Fissile started reading off the pairings, and by the time he finished, no one was listening. Everybody was too busy silently laughing at the pair he'd read right in the middle.

Everyone except me, Trina: Carlos's partner.

# CHAPTER 4
# Secret Undercover Agent

**A**t the Tubs that afternoon, Thea and Donte started off by going on and on about how Mr. Fissile and Ms. Atkinson were so in love and Donte made this gross joke about them sharing a sleeping bag and everyone laughed except for the unhappiest girl in the world.

Don't get me wrong, inside I *knew* why I was Carlos's partner. It was for the same reason that Sara sometimes was, or even David, one of the smart boys in class who was so quiet he might as well not even be there anyway.

"You gotta figure," Sara started, limping ahead of me as we left the Tubs early and walked along the sound barrier, "what are the teachers supposed to do, right?"

"*Mmm,*" I said, which was the first thing I'd even said all afternoon.

"I mean, what, are they going to put him with somebody like Frankie or India?"

"So why don't they just put him with Dr. Johnson as his partner?" I knew I sounded like a pouty little kid right then, but whatever.

Sara shook her head. " 'Cause then he'd never work with anyone, and he's supposed to be part of the class. Ms. Atkinson knows that we can handle it."

And I was like: "What if I don't want to handle it?"

"Tell me about it — I got Frankie as a partner."

"And if I tell my parents, they'll be all like, '*You can handle it, blah blah.*' "

"Parents," Sara said bitterly. "Well, Carlos isn't *always* that bad."

"That's true," I said.

So of course, the next day, My Favorite New Science Partner had another Day After. He didn't even show up until lunchtime, and then he was with Dr. Johnson for music, but then he was around for science and you know it was the worst.

We were measuring our plant experiments. See, Mr. Fissile had us growing these bean plants and putting them in different places to see how they reacted to changes in light. So there were plants shriveling up under desks and in closets, choking on chalk under the blackboard, and getting harassed by mice and who-knows-what under the heaters.

Suddenly there was this *SMASH!*, and we all knew to look right over to Carlos's seat. Sure enough, he was *lying down* on one of the black tables, with his shirt pulled up *AGAIN*, and he was doubled over, like he had been examining his skinny stomach through the small black object — a microscope eyepiece — that he held in his left hand. With his right hand, he was pinching at his belly button, only now he was looking down at the floor, at the big shards of a broken glass beaker that he'd dropped while doing we-don't-want-to-know-what.

"No-ow they're go-ing to ge-et away," Carlos moaned in his shaking Day After voice.

"Carlos!" Mr. Fissile called from across the room, but Carlos didn't move, and so you know that made Mr. Fissile think that he was hurt, and so he dropped one of Latoya's plants and darted between the desks. Mr. Fissile should've known better.

I just sucked my teeth and shook my head, more annoyed than ever. Didn't Carlos know that if he kept this up, some of his classmates might play an elaborate trick on him to get him back for being so annoying?

Mr. Fissile got to Carlos and started helping him down off the desk.

"Watch out for the glass on the floor," he said.

Carlos was looking around like he didn't know where he was, and he was still trying to scratch his stomach with the hand Mr. Fissile was holding. But you know I saw that his other hand was slipping that microscope lens right into his pocket.

"Frankie," Mr. Fissile called as he let go of Carlos and bent down to start picking up the glass shards. "Bring the broom over."

Frankie was over in the corner exactly one foot from where the broom was leaning, but still he got all whiny: "Why do I have to do it? He's the one with the problems!"

Mr. Fissile was crouched on the floor. He sighed, and he sounded so tired I thought he was just going to let it go, but you know he knew he couldn't. He got up with that same overwhelmed look on his face that I'd seen on Ms. Atkinson's, but then he turned to

Frankie and said: "This has nothing to do with you —
it has to do with the broom, which is right next to
you, and we have sharp glass on the floor. Now you
can walk the broom to me or walk yourself to the
board and give yourself a check."

Frankie scowled at the floor, then at the board,
and then grabbed the broom. "Stupid Tweedo," he
mumbled.

Carlos, meanwhile, was turned away toward the
back table like he didn't even remember the glass. It
looked like he was examining his plants, which were
actually growing really well, but I could see that he
was really using the eyepiece to examine the tip of his
index finger.

"You know he stole that, um, magnifier," Frankie
said while we were walking to the Tubs that afternoon. We were halfway up the long steps out of the
T stop, and just like the other stops down here in
Dorchester, it didn't have an elevator. You go to the
nice parts of Boston and you see if they would make a
subway stop without an elevator. So we had to take it
slow for Sara.

Thea: "It's a magnifyING lens."

Donte: "Euuh! It's a magniFIGHTING lens."

"That's not even what I said, Donte!" Thea snapped. "Anyway, it's so totally annoying, it makes me want to just kill him! Did you see him with his shirt up?"

"Yeah, that was gross," I said, not thinking it was *that* gross, but agreeing that his whole big scene had been so annoying.

"Bone belly!" Donte cracked.

"Skeleton Tweedo!" Frankie cracked back.

"God," Thea huffed, "I don't know if I can even wait until the trip!"

"You have to," Sara pointed out, wincing as she hopped up the final two steps, "or you'll get so many checks you won't be able to go."

"True," Thea agreed for once. "Hey, so what's gonna happen with you anyway? I mean, you're too gimpy to go on the trip now, right?"

Sara looked away. "I don't know."

"She's going," I said. "Right, guys? Sara has to go."

"We'll see." Sara — again with that exhausted look on her face.

We walked up Dorchester Avenue in the hot afternoon sun, all of us in our dress-code khaki pants and white shirts and burning up with sweatshirts too because the morning had been cool. The streets around the city were starting to get that summer smell, like the black tar was a frying pan that the trash cooked on all day. Luckily, when we ducked through the torn chain-link fence and arrived behind the warehouse, we found that our tubs were in the shade.

Donte and Frankie tossed around packages of peanut-butter crackers and cartons of chocolate milk, while Thea collected her bet winnings from the day, including my cherry soda. We all scarfed down our snacks and she was still eating her winnings, making us all jealous but secretly just mad that we'd been suckered again.

"Well, everybody," Thea said after drinking down Donte's milk, "another Day After with Carlos, and it was as bad as ever."

"So annoying!" Frankie scowled, kicking the inside of his tub.

"Hey, Trina," Donte called, and I wondered what joke was coming, "I can't believe you have to be his *partner*! That'll teach you for not busting on him more, like us!"

"Whatever!" I snapped.

Frankie piped up: "Maybe now you'll start calling him Tweedo, like we do!"

"I — am — from — Saturn —" Donte said, and he and Frankie both laughed all loud and annoying like boys.

"Why do you guys even call him that anyway?" Sara — glancing up from her secret reading.

"It's from the — the thing — at the . . ." Frankie — trying to think of the word.

"He says he's *visited* by aliens, not that he *is* an alien," Sara said with a scowl.

"Same difference." Donte — scowling even bigger.

I shook my head. "Not really."

Donte: "Why you all defending him now?"

Me: "I'm not."

Thea: "Oh, Trina, you must just want to die."

Sara: "You know you're gonna have to do all the work."

Me: "I can't believe this. It's so unfair!"

"Tell me about it," Sara muttered again, but even grumpier than the day before.

"But Carlos is going to be such a pain!" I shouted. "And he'll get help with all his work, and I'll have to work with that Dr. Johnson, the shrink. . . ."

"Shrink like she's small?" Frankie — not getting it.

"No, Frankie! Shrink like psychologist — like a doctor who studies psychos! And I've seen them through the crack in her office door. She'll be, like,

helping him with tests and giving him juice, and —
and that's not even all! I mean — Sara?"

"*Hmmh?!*" I heard Sara's book fall to the bottom of
her tub as she looked up at me.

"Don't we have a list for this?"

"For what?"

"For all the special things you get to do if you have
problems?"

"Um, oh . . ." She reached down for her backpack
and had a hard time because her big orange cast was
up on the side of her tub. I was just getting up to help
her when she shot a glance over at me that told me she
didn't need help, even though she did. She'd been acting like that a lot this week.

She finally got ahold of her bag and started digging
around. "Right, here it is." And before Sara started
reading I noticed that she didn't take that extra second to feel the spotlight and get everyone's attention.
And when she read she sounded kind of distracted:

"WAYS THAT YOU'RE MORE LUCKY IN SCHOOL
IF YOU HAVE PROBLEMS:

1. You get to miss class all the time.

2. The teacher gives you those
   special, easier versions of things —"

"That's what I'm saying!" Frankie — smiling.

"Shut up!" Thea snapped at him. "You get those for reading AND math!"

"I know. It's better than what you guys have to do."

"Duh, you're not supposed to be proud of it, you SPED!" Donte — calling kids Special Education like he always did, even though we got in huge trouble for it.

"Hey! Never interrupt a list!" I shouted at them, nodding back at Sara.

And then of course Donte had to mock me in his girl's voice: "Never interrupt a list!"

I glared at him. Didn't he see that I was annoyed beyond control right now? That my red beam of anger could swing over and fry him at any moment?

"Okay, anyway," Sara continued:

"3. If you don't do your homework, you can say you didn't get it and you don't have to miss recess.

4. Your special teachers give you extra presents and sundae parties and stuff for doing well, which the rest of us never get.

5. The teachers care more about
   you than everybody else."

"I know, right?" Thea added.

"And that's not all," I said, 'cause it wasn't. "I'll probably do all the work and then watch — we'll get the same grade!"

"It's not *really* the same, though," Thea said, " 'cause Carlos has a SPED record."

"So?" Frankie scowled.

"So," Donte snapped, "they don't look at those the same, duh! He'll have to go to some, like, retarded high school."

Frankie frowned. "Just 'cause he has a SPED record doesn't —"

"Relax, God!" Thea said to Frankie. "Yours is different. Having trouble with reading and math is different than having freak-out problems like Carlos. Besides, you're good at basketball so it don't matter."

"Whatever," I moaned, "I still have to work with him!" Everybody nodded.

"Well, Trina." Thea — sitting up in her tub, which made us sit up a little too: "You know, I just realized that there's one good side to you getting paired up with Carlos. . . ."

"What?"

"You are now, officially, our secret undercover agent, whose mission is to collect all the information that we'll need to TOTALLY trick Carlos!"

"Yeah!" Everybody — nodding.

"Well, I guess that's something good." Me — not feeling good.

"It's perfect," Thea continued. "You can find out exactly what he says about his little *aliens,* and then we'll be able to get him good! Plus, when you go to his house you —"

"Wait! There is no way I am going to his house!"

"Oh, but you have to!" Thea shrugged her shoulders. "Don't you see? That way you can find out what he's all about. Is Tweedo a mama's boy or what? Does he draw pictures of his little alien friends? What does he pretend that they look like? Get it?"

Thea was right, it was perfect for the trick. But that didn't mean I wanted to go. "Well, yeah, I guess, but you guys are going to have to give me a little extra credit, like desserts at lunch and free shots during dodgeball and stuff, 'cause you know this is *REALLY GROSS!*"

"Of course we will." Thea — like she was our queen. Right then I looked at her and felt annoyed. Why did she get to command whatever she wanted? Then I figured I wasn't really annoyed at her, but still at getting Carlos as a partner. This was what I got for being nice, for the guilt-demon: I got the worst partner ever.

"I can't wait for the trick!" Donte shouted, banging his tub with his fists.

Suddenly Sara was lifting herself up. "I have to go," she said. Her face burned as she struggled to get her cast over the side.

"But it's mad early," Frankie whined.

"Hello!" Sara suddenly snapped. "I have a broken ankle, Frankie! God! It takes me twice as long to do everything! I can't just waste my whole afternoon here!"

We were all quiet.

"Besides," she continued, "I can't be late 'cause my mom will freak."

So we left the Tubs, me with my brand-new title as secret undercover agent, and Sara with her bad mood.

I should've felt good about being more critical to a Thea plan than ever before, but as we walked in silence, I only felt trapped.

Carlos was pretty normal for the rest of the week, and on Friday I found him out in the hallway when I was coming back from the bathroom.

No one else was around, so I said: "Hey."

He didn't answer or turn around. He was reading the science bulletin board about designing kites. That was what the eighth graders were doing — any excuse to get them out of the classroom that they were way too big and bored for.

"Carlos."

He flipped through a report that was stapled to the board and when he still didn't look up, I walked right over to him and tapped his shoulder.

"Aah!" He jumped away so fast it surprised me.

"What?"

"Did you feel that?" he asked, panting.

"Feel what?"

"The shock," Carlos said. "Electroshock. Do you know about —" Then his eyes fell. "Oh, never mind." He turned back to the board.

"Know about what?"

He looked up at me again, like he was about to say something, but then he didn't.

"Carlos, you know we're assigned to work on the science project together, right?"

"Yes."

"Well, so, I thought we could, um, get started early."

He was flipping through the paper again. "I know you don't want to work with me."

"Of course I — well — it doesn't matter," I huffed. "We're working together and I want to get a good grade. So, I'll come over sometime to start."

"Come over?" He jumped back again. "Why?!"

"God, relax! It's not like I *want* to."

"But —" he said, looking anywhere but at me, "why don't we just start when Mr. Fissile gives us time next week? Dr. J will be there and —"

"Carlos, of course we'll work then, but I just figured that I'll be, um, going to the library to get books on our topic over the weekend, and then I could, uh, come over on Monday afternoon, and we could get a head start."

He narrowed his eyes at me. "How do you know what our topic is?"

"I don't, but I'll know when I see what books are cool, and —" I stopped because I heard voices behind us. Looking over my shoulder, I saw Frankie and Donte coming down the hall. I turned back to Carlos and spoke louder. "Let me just tell you, it won't be on aliens —"

Carlos jumped at me and grabbed my arm. "You've seen them?!"

I heard Donte gasp behind me, as I yanked my arm away. "Uhh! Get off me, Tweedo!"

He backed off, slouching his shoulders and looking at the ground. "Oh, roger. There I go again. It's just —" He glanced sideways at me. "Never mind."

"So, I'll come over Monday."

"Okay, Katrina."

Now I heard Donte bust out laughing, and I wanted to die. "Oh my God, Carlos! Don't ever call me that, like I'm some ice-skater or something!"

Carlos looked at his feet. "Roger."

"Roger? Is that what you say to the *aliens*?"

"Sometimes," Carlos said, and again, if it was a joke, you would think he would be trying to hold in a laugh, but he looked totally miserable standing there. Then I noticed that he was scratching at the outside of his shirt, and you know I turned and took off.

I heard him call "Bye," and you know Donte and Frankie both cracked up about that too.

"Katrina," I heard Donte say, then start making kissing sounds, but I just brushed by them, my face burning, and got out of there.

# CHAPTER 5
# Tough Times for Sara and Donte

Saturday morning I was sitting at the little table by the window, eating my MMMMM's and watching for Heavyn at the bottom of my bowl. By the way, that bowl was original-issue from back in the day when Heavyn was still with the Divine Divas. If you think about it now, it's funny 'cause at first they were just the Divine Divas and they did everything together and that was that. But then after a while you started to hear about how they weren't getting along and they started doing things like each being at the bottom of their own cereal bowl, instead of all being at the bottom together. Next thing you know, Heavyn split from the group and went solo 'cause she said she needed to be herself. So the bowl was like a sign: Even though it said DIVINE DIVAS under Heavyn's name, she was already on her own.

Across from me was a big wall of newspaper, and behind that was my dad. When we're sitting at the table together, he likes to tell me about all the strange and gross facts that he reads about.

"Listen here," he said from behind the newspaper for, like, the fifth time. "Did you know that eighty-five percent of your body is covered with tiny microscopic creatures?"

"Da! Das so grosh!" I said through a mouthful of chocolaty mush. Actually, I thought it was kind of interesting. One thing that I definitely got from my dad was a sense of curiosity, and like him right now, I couldn't hold it back even when it was annoying, as you'll see later.

He kept going: "And it says . . . uh-oh. They're on your skin, and in your hair, and even —"

"Walter!" Luckily, Mom saved us all by tossing one of her breakfast strawberries from the kitchen, hitting Dad in the head.

"Ooh!" He winced and slapped the paper down on the table. He looked over at her and was about to talk —

"*Mmm-mm*, don't even . . ." Mom said, waving her finger at him, and that was that. She came and sat down. She was in her bathrobe with all these different-colored curlers in her hair. "Headed to the library today?"

"Yuh," I said, wolfing down my MMMMM's.

"So," Dad said, "you're working with that Carlos boy."

"Yeah," I muttered. "It's so unfair. He gets on my nerves."

"Well, honey, I'm sure you can handle being his science partner." And I could just feel another life lesson coming from Dad. "And besides —"

Here it was —

"Someday, when you're older, you'll have to work with all kinds of people you don't like."

"I know." How many times had I heard that? God! "But he's so annoying and he probably won't do any work."

"Well," Mom said, "you know it's situations like this that —"

Oh God, they were going for the double whammy —

"Build character," she finished, and I wanted to die. You know she said that all the time.

"What if I don't need any more character?"

"Trina," Mom said, "you make the best of it with Carlos. You're capable and it's what you need to do."

I was still annoyed by the time I got to the library. What's annoying about Mom, and Dad too, is that no matter what I think of what they're saying, I feel like I *should* be listening to them, like what they're saying is probably true.

The library in our neighborhood is small and old. The carpet is all brown and the shelves are all orange, and it has all these little round wooden tables that always have books all over them because lazy kids like Frankie will get out, like, six books about the same thing and flip through them and then just leave them there. Speaking of Frankie, I found him sitting next to a table all messy with books, and what was he doing? Looking through a comic book.

"God," I huffed, dropping my bag and kicking through his stretched-out legs.

"Whu —" Frankie said. "Somebody brought their problems with them today. . . . Shoot."

I found Sara sitting on the floor way back in the stacks, her crutches leaning against the shelf and her left leg straight out with her orange cast at the end like a lollipop. She was drowning in books.

"Hey," she said without looking up.

"Hey." I sat down next to her. "What are you researching?"

"New Mexico: Roswell, actually." She said it like I should know it.

"What's that?"

"It's this town where aliens crash-landed, like, fifty years ago, and the government covered it up, but everybody who lives there knows it, like, really happened."

"Wow. What did the aliens look like?"

"Well, nobody really knows, 'cause the government hid the bodies, but I think they were the usual kind, with the green skin and the big black eyes — you know, the ones that do most of that visiting and abducting stuff."

"Oh, right. How come you already know so much about this?"

"I read a book about it a couple weeks ago that was written by this army general, who knew the truth but couldn't tell it until he retired."

And remember how I said that Sara was always reading these crazy books? It was always this kind of stuff. Unexplained events, aliens, real monster sightings, and all.

Sara went on, finally looking happy for, like, the first time since the injury. "Our report is going to tell about alien abductions from Roswell to now. It's so cool. Their ships have been seen during wars and stuff, and they, like, practically live in Alaska."

"Wow, this is so you. How is Frankie even going to help at all?"

"He's in charge of researching the effect of all these alien stories on our society, so he's checking out the stories in comic books and on TV, and writing that section. I told him three paragraphs. And get this: Because we're studying aliens, if he ever shoots his mouth off about our little plan for the overnight, people will just think he's talking about something he read for the report, 'cause no one really takes him seriously anyway."

I beamed at her. "That's mad smart."

"And check this out —" Sara reached down by her knee and grabbed a book that was all shimmery green and called *Alien Sightings*. She flipped through to a full-page picture and held it up to me. It showed an alien, all skinny arms and legs in a silver suit, and with this really big green head and huge black eyes.

"Wow, I'd be freaked if that thing ever showed up to take me."

"I know, right? But this is a kid in a costume. I bet we can get costumes like this in the Theater District."

"Oh my God, that would be so awesome! We could go with my stepsister, Darcelle. She goes down to Chinatown on Saturdays. I go with her sometimes."

"Just think: Masks like that, if we had them, we'd be so scary, right?"

"Yeah . . ." And we shared our look like we knew everything. Then for a second, I was almost a little nervous. Usually it was me who was more into Thea's plans than Sara, but she seemed really into this. And it was getting big too. I mean, renting costumes just to trick a kid? It was nice to see her smile about *something*, though, so that made me feel good.

I got up and wandered around the stacks until I finally found the perfect science project topic for Carlos and me: *Predators of the Serengeti.*

Even a weirdo like Carlos would have to like researching bloodthirsty African animals. I flipped through the book, which had lots of big color pictures. Looking at the lions feasting on zebra bones, I got a little excited, then remembered that I was still annoyed.

When I got back to Sara's aisle, she had a stack of books under her arm and was trying to stand up by leaning on one of her crutches.

"Here, let me help —"

But suddenly Sara slipped and came down right on her lollipop leg. "Oww! Damn!" She gnashed her teeth together.

"Are you okay?" I knelt down beside her.

"No!" she hissed. "What do you think already?" Her face was bright pink. She winced and little tears leaked from the sides of her eyes.

"This so totally sucks," she muttered.

"I know —"

"No you don't!" Sara — snapping like she never did. "Nobody does. I was supposed to be swimming this morning! That's one more meet that I missed. I'll never get back in shape in time to qualify for Arizona. Some summer . . ."

"Well," I tried, "at least you can, like, hang out around here for a change."

"Oh yeah, great," she said, "what's that gonna be like? Going to the movies and sweating at the Tubs? Where's *that* going to get me?"

"I don't know." I could tell it was time to back off a

bit 'cause Sara, she didn't even notice that she was talking about *my* summer.

"And my dad went to the meet this morning without me, to *'check out the competition,'* he said. Hello! I'm not even there! They totally think it's my fault, like I screwed up so bad, when it was just an accident."

I had no idea what to say about that, so I just picked up her books. "Come on. Let's get you back over to where you can sit and feel better."

But Sara didn't feel better. She barely talked for the rest of the day.

So the next Monday, two weeks before the overnight, it was time to go to Carlos's house.

I waited until he had already left school, and then until everyone else was gone, before I headed across the parking lot, turning left outside the gate instead of my usual right. Even though everybody knew I was going, I still didn't want to be seen. It didn't matter that my friends knew this was a secret mission. They would *still* make fun of me if they saw me. And I hadn't even gone five steps when I was caught.

"Trina!" I turned around and saw Donte calling to me from the steps. I huffed and stomped my feet and basically wanted to die. "Wait up!"

He was running across the parking lot with that silly, empty backpack on wheels bouncing this way and that at his heels. Donte is not the most athletic kid in school. He's a little heavy, so he's not too fast, and he's not too tall. He's not the kind of kid who gets picked last, but he is the kind of kid who gets picked *almost* last, just before that imaginary line that separates the kids who *always* get picked last. I think Donte knows how close he is to that line, and that's why he is so hard on the losers, 'cause that way you'll think he isn't one of them. And once Donte is on the team, he usually just kind of drifts around, like in the middle of the football field or at the other end of the basketball court. Kids like Frankie, who can *play*, get in his face because he's lazy on defense.

He pulled up next to me, all out of breath. "You — uh, going to — the weirdo's house, eh?"

"Yeah." I turned and started walking fast. "So you can just get on with it, making fun of me and all." But what was strange was that Donte turned and walked next to me, even though his house was the other way.

What was stranger was that he didn't crack any jokes, about Carlos, or Katrina, or anything. It made me wonder if something was wrong with him.

"So what did you do to get kept after school?" I asked him.

"Whatever, I didn't do nothin', stupid Ms. Atkinson." Donte — saying what he always said.

"How many checks did you get?"

"One, but I don't care — stupid school makes me sick."

"*Mm-hmm.*" I nodded — this was the usual Donte-after-getting-in-trouble stuff.

"I'm glad I'm leaving."

"Yyyup — wait, what?" I stopped and turned and when he tried to keep walking, I grabbed his arm and spun him back around. "What are you talking about?"

Donte looked away. "Oh. Nothing."

"Tell me."

He sighed. "My mom got me into St. Anthony's Academy."

"Where your sister goes?" I knew Donte's younger sister had gotten into St. Anthony's last year and that Donte had been on the waiting list, but so was, like, half the school.

"Yeah. Mom told me this weekend after I came back from Dad's. You'd better not tell anyone."

"Oh my God, I won't. But — so you're really leaving?"

"End of the year." He looked down at the ground. Then he looked back up and, you know, he maybe looked sad, but like a boy, he wasn't going to show it. "It's about time, 'cause I hate this stupid school anyway!"

I started walking again, not really knowing what to say. If I was Donte, I would have been worried about going to St. Anthony's. I mean, it's not an exam school or anything, but it's tough, and he wouldn't be able to get away with doing nothing like he always did here.

"Teachers here get on my nerves," Donte said, "always acting like they know everything when they're not even any older than my mother. At St. Anthony's, the teachers are old and, like, experts on their subjects."

"*Mmm-hmm.*"

"And on Fridays, they get to dress down and the eighth graders get to go out for lunch —"

"Kind of like how we get free period."

"Theirs is better, not boring like here."

*"Mmm . . ."*

We walked along silently. Carlos only lived two blocks from school, on a street that just looked like your parents wouldn't want you on it at night. I stopped at the corner and Donte, who was busy staring at the sidewalk, kept going for a second before he noticed.

"This is where Carlos lives," I said. "So, I'll see you tomorrow?"

"Right," he said.

"I suppose you're going to make fun of me for having to go here."

"Nah, whatever," Donte said, walking away with his head down. "That's stupid."

I watched Donte go, wondering: Was he really sad about leaving and just acting like he wasn't? There was this kid Denzel who left at the end of fifth grade, and for the last month of school he was so mean and nasty that everybody was glad to see him go. Then on the last day of school, he was all crying about every little thing and wouldn't talk to anyone. It was like if everyone thought you were a jerk, then it would be easier to leave. I hoped that wasn't Donte's plan.

He disappeared up the road, and I shrugged and turned down Carlos's street.

# CHAPTER 6
# The Severed Heads
# Where the Aliens Live

I t was a hot, sunny afternoon, and Carlos's street
was alive like streets in our neighborhood will be
if it's warm enough. Each tall, boxy three-family
house had its front door hanging open and there were
kids crawling all over the front porches. Cars were
parked along both sides of the street, and out in the
middle, like ten kids were playing football, all with
their shirts off and shorts hanging down so low you
could see their boxers. And you could tell which kid
thought he was the best, because he was barefoot and
his cut-off shorts were, like, barely even on. On the
sidewalk there were two kids in hula hoops, a couple
kids darting around on scooters, and a couple older

girls with little ones climbing all over them. Someone had speakers blaring out of an upstairs window, and so the whole street had its own slow beat. When the breeze kicked up, there was that street-griddle smell again. And you know, when you put all that together — it was nice.

Carlos's house was just past the football game. It was dark brown with three yellow porches sagging off the front. The little square of front yard had a chain-link fence around it. Inside, all the grass was wild and tall and there were plastic toys like tricycles and dump trucks just lying around with their colors all faded by the sun.

I pushed through the squeaky gate and walked up the creaky steps. I rang the bell but there was no answer. Then I heard a screen door bang from up on the porches.

"Hello?" I heard from up there.

I hopped down the stairs and saw little Carlos up on the top porch.

"I'll be right down!" he said. I walked back up to the door and just started praying that when he came down he'd have a shirt on, 'cause he didn't just then and it was *REALLY GROSS*.

Luckily, when the door opened, he did. At least at school, with his dress-code clothes on, Carlos looked like, even if you might doubt it, he must be in middle school. But here, standing in the doorway with his scrawny little body in a little green T-shirt and long jean cut-offs and with his little bare feet and knobby knees and bony arms, he looked like he might be in fourth grade.

"Hi," he said, looking behind me to the left, then the right. "Are you alone?"

"Of course I'm alone. Who would want to come here with me?"

"Yeah, I guess," he agreed.

"So are we going in or what?"

"Oh — are we going in? Yes! Yes, we are, come on."

I followed him in, then he ducked behind me to close and bolt the door. He jumped ahead again and started up the narrow, sagging staircase that had this gold carpet that was all worn up the middle. We got to the landing of the second floor and the bass in that apartment was making the walls shake. It sounded like a Heavyn song, but the bass was so loud that I couldn't even tell, which made me know it was some boy listening in there. Boys and their bass. God!

We got up to the third floor and Carlos knocked on the door. The bass from downstairs was still rumbling our feet.

"It's me again!" he called in his little voice.

There were creaking footsteps and then the sound of locks clicking open, and a young woman, like eighteen, let us in.

"Thanks, Alexis, this is Trina, the girl from school. Trina, this is my cousin Alexis."

"Hey," Alexis said like I wasn't even close to as interesting as the pink hairbrush she had in her hand.

"Nice to meet you," I said before I could stop my stupid manners from making me sound like a loser, but Alexis had already turned and walked back over to a big old yellow-and-white-flowered couch, where a little girl, like a younger sister or a daughter or something, was sitting with a white plastic doll, chewing on its rubber head and watching TV.

"That's Kasey, my sister," Carlos said as he walked across the room. "Come on."

The whole place smelled like burnt sugar. I followed Carlos across the living room, past the doorway to the kitchen, where I saw a bent pan of what I guessed was supposed to be brownies lying on the stove. We headed down a narrow hallway, past the bathroom, which smelled like a pool, and I noticed a plastic bottle of blue liquid just sitting open on the counter, a sponge beside it.

"You clean this place yourself?" I asked Carlos, wrinkling my nose.

"Yeah, I just cleaned the bathroom. Smells good, right? And before you came I made brownies that we can eat later."

"Uh, that's okay. I might not be hungry."

Carlos pushed open a door at the end of the hall and I followed him into a bedroom that even made mine look big. There were two beds. The one under the window was clearly Carlos's — I could tell by the bedspread with baseballs and footballs and soccer balls all over it. The other was really narrow and short and had a railing around the sides. It was against the far wall, next to the closets, which had these brown sliding doors. One of them was off its track.

"This is me and Kasey's room. Kasey's three."

"Does your cousin live here too?"

"No, she just babysits when my mom's working a double shift. Alexis has an audition for a modeling agency in Quincy and —"

But I cut him off. "Listen, Carlos, I think we should get our work done kinda fast, okay? I have a lot of homework and I can't be here all afternoon."

"Oh, roger."

Carlos dropped down on a yellow beanbag in the middle of this little round carpet that was covered with, you guessed it: a map of the solar system. He leaned toward me. "So, what's our topic?"

"African predators," I said, sitting on the edge of his bed and pulling the book, a video, and a notebook out of my backpack. "Like lions and leopards and cheetahs —"

"And tigers, yeah I know." Carlos slouched his shoulders and looked away like he was maybe the only boy in the world who didn't think that was cool.

"Actually, tigers don't live in Africa, but why do you sound like you don't like the topic, not like you have a choice?"

"Do I? Oh no, it's fine."

"Good. I mean, it better be. Now, listen, Carlos: Your job is to watch this and to take notes." I tossed the video to him. "I got this book and it has cool information. Like, did you know that lions can move so slowly and quietly that they can get to be, like, only ten feet away from an antelope before they're even detected? That way they don't have to run as far. And — what?"

'Cause Carlos, he wasn't even listening to me. Instead, he was just staring out the window. He turned back and shook his head. "Oh, huh? Nothing, I —" And then I couldn't even believe it, because he started scratching at his stomach with his left hand, and his right started scratching the left's elbow.

I jumped up. "Okay, gross!"

"What?"

"Duh, the scratching!"

"What's wrong with scratching? I get rashes, like from if I drink milk and stuff."

"Well . . ." I started to sit back down. "I guess that's kind of normal." I flipped open the book on the Serengeti. "Anyway, it says here that hyenas always hunt in packs. Hey, remember those hyenas that were at the Franklin Park Zoo two years ago? We went with Ms. Wilson."

"I didn't go."

"Oh. But you've seen them, right?"

"I've never been to the zoo."

"Really?" I kind of couldn't believe that. "But it's right around the corner."

"It's boring. I — I like doing other things." Carlos

turned the video over in his hands like it was the most uninteresting thing in the world. "Is it long?"

"No." I was still trying to get over the fact that he thought the zoo was boring. "It's only, like, a half hour."

"I hope it's not boring."

"How can it be boring, Carlos? It's about animals hunting and killing each other! There's blood! Guts being eaten! God!" I threw up my hands. "Are you a boy or what?"

"Yeah."

"Well, duh. So you have to like the video."

I flipped through my book again, looking for another example to convince him. "Okay, here, check this out: Leopards, right, they will sit in a tree and watch their prey and actually get to know them. After a while, the gazelle forgets the leopard is even there. Then it wanders too close, and *wham!*, the leopard leaps down, grabs it by the throat, and drags it all the way back into the tree to let it die and then eat it. Now, if that's not as interesting as science can be, I don't know what is. Here, check out the picture."

I passed the book to Carlos. He dropped it in his lap and looked at the picture of the leopard with the little gazelle in its jaws. I looked around his room now, playing my part as secret agent, and noticed that the walls were plastered with drawings, most of them in pencil on lined paper. They looked like mountains, and symbols, and little figures.

Carlos flipped the page to a picture of the leopard leaping out of the branches right onto the little gazelle. "How come he doesn't go after the bigger ones that have more meat?"

"Because," I said, "it's too hard to catch a big one. The littlest ones are the weakest, and the easiest to surprise, not to mention carry into a tree. It's survival of the fittest. Only the strongest of the species survive."

"Oh . . ." He closed the book and handed it back to me.

And sitting there, looking down at Carlos from up on the bed, the guilt-demon made my stomach shiver with a strange thought: What if Carlos was the gazelle, and here I was, the leopard, letting him forget I was dangerous, all the while planning a trick on him?

The feeling just made me want to leave. We'd done all we needed to do for the report for now. I hadn't gotten any info yet for the trick, but I couldn't think of anything to ask. I didn't even *want* to ask any-thing. So instead, I packed the book into my bag.

"So," I said, getting up to go, "you watch the video and take notes, okay?"

"You're leaving already?" Carlos asked. "But don't you want a brownie?"

"Um, no thanks. You can have them all." I turned to the door. "I'm really not —"

"Trina?"

I turned back to find Carlos looking up at me with huge eyes. "What?"

He looked away, then started scratching his left knee. "Um —"

"God, Carlos, what is it? And you're scratching again!"

"Oh!" He looked down at his hand and leg like they didn't belong to him. "Sorry."

"So what is it already?"

Carlos looked sideways at me. He sounded like he was holding his breath when he spoke. "Can I show you something?"

And you know, what's annoying about me is what I did right then: Even though I just wanted to get out of there, what did I have to go and say? "What do you want to show me?"

Carlos looked left and right, like to see if anyone was listening. *"Them."*

"Do you mean your *aliens*?" I huffed, even though this was perfect for the trick. But then I heard myself saying: "Carlos, don't you know how annoying it is whenever you do this whole big act? Do you think it makes you cool or something? Do you think it will make people like you?"

"Do I think they'll like me?" Carlos suddenly jumped up to his feet. "No! I think it will make everyone hate me, but I can't help it!" He walked over by the window.

"I just don't get why you do it," I said.

"I don't mean to!" he said. His voice became a squeak. "It — it's just what happens."

And again I had that question: If his problems were an act, then why did Carlos look so miserable? And besides, remember what I said about that sense of curiosity that I got from my dad? Well, this was one of those times that I just couldn't stop it. And next thing I knew, I was saying: "All right, Carlos, fine. Show me, then."

Carlos looked up again: "Really?"

"Yes already!"

"Cool!" Carlos scurried over to the foot of his bed. He reached down in the tight, cluttered corner between the ends of the two beds. "Right . . . here . . ."

he grunted, picking up a big purple basket of mixed-up toys and dropping it on his bed. Then he reached down so his head disappeared. When he stood up, his arms were wrapped around a small glass aquarium.

"Um . . . the *aliens* fit inside that thing?" Me — playing along now.

"Oh yeah."

"I'm afraid to ask how many you have in there."

"Oh, a bunch, like fifty I think, last time I counted."

I stared at the aquarium, honestly not knowing what to say to that. It had a wire-mesh top, like the kind that Mr. Fissile had on his turtle tank. Inside, Carlos had spread white sand across the bottom and laid down two long, flat rocks, one leaning on the other. There was a fake plant, all long with tiny leaves, that I knew I'd seen before.

"Hey," I said as he wobbled back and forth, struggling to get the heavy little tank to the middle of the floor, "that's one of those plants from Mr. Fissile's goldfish t —"

But then I saw what else was in the tank, and not only did I not finish, I almost screamed. Scattered all over the sand were little heads. For one horrified second I didn't know what they were, then I got it: doll heads. The rubber kind that would come on plastic dolls, like the one that Carlos's sister had been chewing. Little chewed-up heads, popped off at the neck and hollow inside. You could tell that some of them used to have hair too, but that was long gone. Most of the paint had flaked off their mangled faces, and so the eye colors, lip colors, and hair were splotchy with the peachy-colored rubber beneath.

Carlos collapsed to the floor, putting the tank on the beanbag.

"That is twisted," I said, even as I was kneeling down to get a closer look. "Your sister's a psycho doll killer."

"Ooh! Wait!" Carlos leaped up again and raced around me, back to his bed, where he stuck his arm underneath the mattress and started digging around.

I kept looking into the tank. Other than rubber heads, I didn't see anything. "There's nothing in here —"

"*Shshsh!*" Carlos hissed at me. "You'll wake them!" He pulled his skinny arm out and flipped a small black object up into the air.

"Man, Carlos," I said, recognizing the microscope eyepiece right away, "how many things have you stolen from Mr. Fissile's room anyway?"

"Only three of these," he said, throwing his shoulders back for just a second like he was all proud, but right away he sagged. "I always break them." He grabbed another object from under the bed, then dropped down next to me again. "Here." He handed me a stolen plastic magnifying glass. "You use this. The eyepieces are harder to use and I've had more experience."

"Okay . . ." I couldn't believe he was acting so serious about this. "So, um, what's with the heads?"

Carlos took the top off the tank and slowly reached down, picking up a little blond head with its face chewed away. "*They* like dark places, so I got Kasey to give me these."

He raised the head and shook it, frowning as nothing came out of the neck. He dropped it and picked up another one. "Now listen, Trina: They're really fast, so when we see them, I'll get out of the way so that you can look in and see."

"All right." And you know, sitting there I was actually getting a little nervous. I mean, of course he was lying, but still . . .

"Rats." Now Carlos was getting frustrated, because he'd shaken four heads and nothing had come out. He shook three more empty ones viciously, slamming the last one against the side of the tank. There was only one more to check.

I sat back, my curiosity spell starting to wear off. "Carlos, I can't believe you're trying to make me think you really have aliens inside doll heads inside a fish tank."

He shook the last empty head. "They were here this morning — shoot!" He threw the microscope lens across the room. It cracked against the wall and fell behind Kasey's bed.

"No wonder you break them all the time."

Carlos looked to the window. "They must've teleported when they heard you come in."

"Ha." I couldn't believe he wanted to keep up with it. "Why would *they* do that?"

"Because they don't want to be discovered. No one is supposed to know they're here."

"*You* know."

"That's because they're using me. I'm their test subject!"

"You . . ." Now this was going too far. I almost laughed. "Okay," I said, standing, "I'm really leaving now."

"Oh," Carlos moaned, slapping the top back on the aquarium. "Now you think I'm a freak."

"Uh . . ." I decided to leave that one alone. "Listen, you just watch that video, and I'll come over again next week."

"Again!?" Carlos asked. "Why don't we just do it during class, when Dr. J is there? She helps me."

"Well, see," I tried to think of an excuse, "I think we'll need extra time to, uh, make our report the best it can be."

"Oh. Roger." Carlos stood up. "Trina," he said, his voice getting extra small.

You know how sometimes you can just tell when someone wants to say something, like, nice to you, and you get that nervous feeling because you just *know* you should run before it happens? Well, that's how I felt, but I was too slow.

Carlos was standing with his hands behind his back. "Thanks for looking at my aliens, even though they ran off again."

I almost said, *Thanks for showing me,* but then I stopped myself. "Whatever. I just —"

But he cut me off. "Thanks for believing that they were real."

"Carlos!" I felt so yucky all of a sudden, and you know I couldn't help what I said next: "Except I don't believe in them. God!" I turned and rushed out his door.

"Thanks anyway!" he called.

I stopped and turned back around and was like: "Listen, whatever you do, don't even think about telling anyone that you tried to show me your little pet *alien* collection."

His face went blank. "Roger."

"Good." As I walked down the hall my heart slowed, but I didn't feel better. I could feel the guilt-demon working away on my stomach.

I let myself out. Outside, the street was loud and everything was blurry in the hot yellow afternoon. I had just reached the sidewalk when I heard Carlos from up on the porch:

"See you tomorrow, Trina!"

I looked up, and he was waving.

I turned back around, not waving — but it was way too late.

"Aww, look, Carlos finally got a girl!"

"He's a playa!"

"Our little bro's finally getting some! Hey, girl!"

I kept my head down and walked faster.

"Hey, girl, how's our little man treating you?"

" 'Cause you know I could treat you better!"

By the time I got to the corner, they were playing their game again and forgetting all about me. But I felt lame and embarrassed all the way home. For the rest of the day I thought about Carlos. I still felt bad for me, for being his partner — but I felt good about getting info for the trick — but then I also felt bad for him again, because he had to deal with himself, and his life, which just seemed kinda lonely and sad.

# CHAPTER 7
# Amazing Frank's Costume Shop

The next day we had recess at the nearby park instead of in the school parking lot, and I ended up sitting alone at the top of the highest tower of the jungle gym. I was above the suspension bridge and ladders and slides, on a platform with a roof over it so you could be out of the hot, hazy June sun and away from annoying boys. Because Donte, just like the stupid jerk that he was, totally harassed me about going to Carlos's house all morning, even though he said he wouldn't.

I sat up there, watching my class, feeling bad. Everyone else was pretty much just sitting around too, 'cause we all thought the park was for babies. Even the stupid boys, who would always play football in the parking lot at school, they never played on this nice big field.

So I got about ten seconds of peace and quiet before Donte's big head appeared, with Frankie's beside him. "Did you see his bed?" Donte said.

"*Ohh!*" Frankie shouted.

"God!" I jumped up and moved to the far corner of the platform. "You're so gross! And you're a jerk, 'cause you said you wouldn't make fun of me."

"Whatever." Donte — making a face like he was tasting the brown mush they called spinach in the school lunches. "Like I'm some girlfriend of yours or something."

"You're both stupid."

"Yup." Donte's head looked over at Frankie's head. "It's like I said, Trina *likes* Carlos. She wants to *research* him —"

"Donte!"

"She wants to touch his alien!"

"*Ohh!*"

"I hate you! God!" And I did. Stupid, stupid Donte! And you know the worst part was that I was so mad I was starting to cry.

"Ha," Donte said, "she always thinks she's so much better than us, but she's just a baby —"

"SHUT UP!" Me — an idiot who only knew two words.

"It's about time she — ahh!"

And like the answer to my dreams, Donte's head suddenly dropped out of sight.

Frankie looked down. "Whoa, Donte, you've got problems now —"

And Donte's head was replaced by Thea's head. And the way she looked at Frankie, you know he jumped right off that ladder, because if he didn't, he *knew what would happen*. Then she pulled her big self up onto the platform. I sat down in the corner and brushed at my tears with my forearm.

"Girl." Thea knelt down beside me and rubbed my back. "Forget about them. Don't you remember, there are two ways that boys always let you know it's June? One: They smell so bad the whole classroom starts to stink, and two: They act like even bigger jerks than in May. And man, that Donte stinks!"

"He's just being a jerk 'cause he's scared about leaving."

"Leaving where?"

"Oh —" Suddenly I felt like my mouth was a mile too big. If Thea didn't know, then Donte really hadn't told anyone else. "Just, I mean, on summer vacation."

And what's annoying about me is that right there: I was mad at Donte, and I knew that telling Thea would be such a sweet way to get revenge, and I didn't. Because I knew he didn't want anyone to know, and he trusted me to keep the secret. Sometimes I annoy me so much!

Thea waved her hand. "Whatever. Who cares about him? What did you find out at Carlos's?"

I wiped my face off. You know, I kinda didn't feel like saying anything. "Well . . ." I could feel my stomach getting tighter, like a rope in a tug-of-war. There was Thea, and the plan and everything related to my very existence at school on the one end of the rope, and on the other was little Carlos and the guilt-demon. But right then, it was bad enough me being weak and crying 'cause of Donte — I wasn't going to be weak about the plan too. "Wait, where is he?"

Thea looked around, then pointed. "Down there."

Carlos was down by the fence behind the swings, sitting in the shade, too small as usual, examining a pile of sand in the palm of his hand with one of those stolen microscope eyepieces.

"Right, well." I sniffed back the last of my stuffy, crying nose. "First of all, he has an *alien* collection in this aquarium. . . ." I told her most of it, but left out some of the weirdest details, like the doll heads, because Thea didn't need to know *everything*.

"Good work," Thea said, getting up. "This is going to be so fun." She started climbing back down a ladder. "Oh, and do you want me to do anything else to Donte after I punch him?"

"No, that's enough."

"Are you sure? 'Cause that punch is just from me. How about if I trip him on the way back to school, and that can be from you?"

"Okay."

I sat there for a while and caught my breath and retied my braids. After a minute or two I heard Donte cry out 'cause Thea had socked him in the shoulder.

You know, I didn't feel a whole lot better. It was weird with Thea — you might think that it was nice to have her being all, like, really nice to me like she just was, but it wasn't all that nice, because this kind of thing only happened when we were getting ready to do a trick. Weeks could go by where Thea and I would never really get into each other's business other than at the Tubs. If Sara had been up there in the jungle gym, that would have been different, 'cause she and I talked about everything we were upset about all the time. With Thea, sometimes I just felt like I only mattered to her if she needed something from me.

And speaking of Sara, that's what made talking to Thea weirder. I *should* have been talking to Sara. She *should* have been up here with me, but instead, she was down on a bench with Ms. Atkinson. We hadn't talked much all week. She seemed more down and depressed with every day. At first it didn't bother me, but then on Saturday, when we finally went to the costume shop, it sure did.

Saturday was the hottest June day yet, a day when you were starting to sweat before you finished drying off after a shower — one of those days that had that little scent of salt and dead fish from the harbor whenever the breeze blew just right.

What's great about my stepsister, Darcelle, is that whenever she takes me somewhere, she always lets me help her with her newspaper story. She writes for the *Community News* and was writing a series of stories about businesses trying to survive in the Chinatown part of Boston. Whenever I went along with her, she let me walk around the nearby blocks and take notes about what interesting places she could maybe write about next. She says I have a good eye for detail.

I had to get up early, and they were sitting at the table having coffee when I walked in. Darcelle is tall like my mom, and both of them are taller than my dad. Sometimes Darcelle leans down when my dad is talking, pretending that it's hard to hear what he's saying, and you know my mom gets such a kick out of that.

"Morning, Trina," Darcelle said, checking her watch. "It's about time."

"I got up so early!"

"I know, I know. I remember being young and irresponsible."

"I'll bet you do," Mom said with a laugh into her mug. She was dressed on a Saturday morning for a change.

I guess we all liked to look good for Darcelle because she always looked so stylish and put together. She had straightened her hair since the last time I'd seen her, added red streaks, and had it back with a headband of gold fabric. It was those kinds of details that she always got right.

"Well, are you ready to go or what?" She was standing up, grabbing her black bag from the couch.

"Yeah."

"Hope you have your notebook."

"Of course." I patted my sky-blue bag just to show that I certainly did have the soft corduroy journal that she'd given me.

The costume shop that Sara and I were going to go to was actually about three blocks away from Chinatown, toward the Theater District, which was a little farther than Darcelle would want me to go, but I figured I would just tell her about it when we met up with her afterward, and then say we didn't realize how far we'd gone. I didn't really think she'd mind anyway. She trusted me.

We picked up Sara, and she didn't have her crutches. Her cast was off too, and instead she was wearing this smaller blue air-brace thing. You'd think that would've put her in a better mood, but no.

I could tell as soon as I tried to get the door for her and she just reached by me and did it herself. "Is it getting better?" I asked.

"Yeah," she muttered, "but I'm going to be wearing this for, like, three more weeks."

"But maybe now you can come on the overnight?"

"Maybe. My parents are still talking it over."

We got in the car, and Sara didn't speak. She didn't

even say hello to Darcelle, and that was not like Sara. And you know, like, when you can just tell that someone is in a bad mood, but you, like, try really hard to be all in a good mood and start a conversation in a good way, even though the whole moment feels like a ticking bomb? Well, that was me with Sara. I pulled out a list we started the other day, hoping that would help.

"So I brought that list . . ."

Sara just stared out the window.

"Hey, Sara," Darcelle said, looking at her in the mirror.

"Oh, hi," she said back finally.

"Let's see. . . ." Me — still trying. "Where were we? Oh yeah —" I started reading:

### "REASONS WHY WE KNOW THAT MR. FISSILE AND MS. ATKINSON ARE, LIKE, TOTALLY IN LOVE:

1. They are both white, and, like, thirty, so they're all old and desperate, and they work together.

2. If you get sent upstairs from art or music, you will totally find them sitting together in the kitchen

both eating at the same time and talking.

3. Whenever they're in the hall, like, getting on some kid's case, they do that annoying thing where they talk to each other about the kid like he's not even there, even though he's right there, and they go back and forth, and whenever one of them is talking, the other is staring back with big dopey eyes like even though they're saying all this stuff, they're secretly just saying, 'I *love* you,' and 'I *love* you too.'

4. This one time, when we were staying after school in Ms. Atkinson's writing group, Mr. Fissile popped in, and he didn't know we'd be there, and he called her Tracy, and that's, like, her first name, and that's *REALLY GROSS.*"

I twisted around to see Sara. "So we need one more. What do you think?"

"I don't know." Sara — like a ticking bomb.

"How about when we caught him taking a sip of

her soda at the dance that one time?" Silly me — still trying.

"That's stupid," she said, still looking out the window. "They're not even in love. I mean, we've met Ms. Atkinson's boyfriend, don't you remember?"

And I knew by the way Sara said it that this was just the way it was going to be and that made me mad. My one day with Darcelle, and I invited Sara along, and this was how she acted?

It wasn't until we had parked, and Sara and I were on our own, that I was finally like: "What's with you?"

"Nothing." She walked along, grimacing with almost every step. "My ankle hurts. I'm not supposed to be walking on it this much, but I'm sick of sitting around all the time."

"I bet you're getting a lot of reading done," I tried.

"I'm sick of reading. My parents are all on my case about school even more than usual. They act like because I can't swim I'm suddenly going to become some failure in everything."

"Huh." Once again, I wasn't sure what else to say to that. We kept walking, and rounded the corner onto Hudson Street. "It should be up here on the left."

Amazing Frank's Costume Shop was the first one listed online, and it had a huge ad, so that was good, 'cause when you're sneaking onto the Internet during computer class, you have to work fast. We saw the enormous pink sign with yellow letters as we rounded the corner. Its two front windows were surrounded in red chili pepper lights that blinked on and off, chasing each other around the window.

Sara and I stopped and just stared. The left window had three shelves of masks on white Styrofoam heads: werewolves, Frankensteins, twisted demons with their eyeballs hanging out and bloody gashes all over their faces, a pig mask — that might have been the scariest one of all, 'cause you know pigs are kind of freaky — pirate masks and big felt hats with feathers sticking out of them, helmets for astronauts, Vikings, demon football players, and androids. The right-side window had a long rack of hanging costumes: ball gowns, black robes, a bloody bride dress, a suit of armor, a big, puffy, and very corny purple medieval costume, and even a big old brown suit like a deep-sea diver would wear.

I looked over at Sara and finally she grinned. "This is totally the place," she said.

We walked inside. The store was busy and without

air-conditioning, so the whole place smelled stuffy like mothballs, but then also like sweat and perfume and deodorant and dampness, so much so that I almost passed out. To our left we passed the mask section, and then aisles of hair coloring and fake parts, like mustaches, beards, wigs, hands, and then some other body parts that I can't even write down, but I'm sure you can imagine what they were. And down the right wall there were just racks and racks of costumes.

I checked my watch. We had twenty minutes more before we needed to be back. "We'd better ask," I whispered, even though it was so loud in there, with punk music blasting.

We walked up to the long glass counter and got in line behind this really tall and skinny bald guy who was wearing a white tank top and these leathery purple pants like he was a girl going out to a club. Sara and I rolled our eyes at each other. When he turned to leave, we saw that he had a pink cat in his arms that was either fake or dead and stuffed, and either way what was up with that? He also had a silver star painted around his right eye.

Leaning on the counter was this big woman with dyed black hair and thick black rectangle glasses.

She had on a tight purple T-shirt with orange at the collar and the sleeves. The shirt said: *I only ACT like I care.* A button on her shirt read: *I'm Frank Today.*

"What's up, ladies?" she said around the mouthful of gum that she was smacking on.

I suddenly felt like leaving. But you know Sara — she might have been a pill lately, but this was one of those times in life where she got that look like the spotlight was shining right on her.

"We're looking for alien costumes for our school's end-of-the-year production," she said, even putting a finger in her hair and twisting it a little bit so that she looked kinda bored.

"Oh yeah, what play?" the woman said, still chomping. Now she twisted at her hair too and I wondered if this was like some kind of little battle that actor types had, to see who could look like they cared the least.

But now that I finally saw that light back on Sara, I knew how to play along. "You wouldn't know it," I said, looking over at the body parts. "It's new."

"Honey, I only wouldn't know it if it sucks."

And back and forth we went, all smiling, until

Frank Today pointed us toward the alien costumes: "Head down past zombies, turn right after the Hamlet Zone, and you'll see the Aisle of Abduction just after that."

"Thanks!" we both finished together.

After fifteen minutes of picking through alien costumes, then trying on astronaut helmets, werewolf masks, princess gowns, and psycho-killer straitjackets, and finally having fun like we used to, we were back outside. We had a purple plastic Amazing Frank's bag full of two sparkly silver suits with gold boots, two green rubber alien heads with black mesh eyes, two sets of gloves with extra-long rubbery fingers, and, the best part of all, an inflatable flying saucer. When you blew it up, it would be, like, three feet across, which wasn't all that big, but still, it had battery-powered blinking lights and came with a pulley and rope. The idea was that you could make it seem like a flying saucer was going by high up in the sky.

"This stuff is so perfect." I said. "Definitely worth both our allowances put together." I started speeding up the street, then realized that Sara wasn't next to me. I turned around to see her stopped on the sidewalk, her face getting red. "You okay?" I called back to her.

"Fine," she said like you knew she wasn't, with her teeth gritted and not looking at me. That smile I saw back in the store was already gone, and that bad-mood cloud was back.

I checked my watch. It was official — we were going to be late unless we hurried. We had a ten-minute walk and only five minutes to do it in. "Hey," I called to her, trying to sound calm but really feeling so stressed because I did *not* want to disappoint Darcelle. "We've got to hurry."

And you know how sometimes you say something, and even while it's coming out of your mouth you just know that you shouldn't be saying it? Well, this was one of those times, 'cause Sara gave me *that look*. "Too bad," she said under her breath, and I totally heard her.

"What?"

"Nothing." She brushed by me. "You said we had to hurry so let's go."

But you know what? That was it. Two weeks of this from her, and I wasn't taking it anymore. "You know, Sara, I know you're upset about your ankle and swimming but —"

She spun around. "It's not about the swimming!" She looked mad like I'd never seen her.

"Yeah, right! Then what is it about?"

"Everything! Why can't you just let me be upset?"

"Because you're my friend and it's annoying!"

"Ugh! You don't get it."

I stepped right in front of her. "What don't I *get*?"

Sara looked right at me and threw up her hands. "How would you understand what it's like anyway? To do what I do —"

"Like what?"

"Like what I do every day! And swimming in the Junior Olympics! I can't afford to just be normal! I have to be perfect all the time and this broken ankle is ruining everything!"

"Sara, who ever said you had to be perfect all the time?"

"Nobody, I — you don't get it!" Tears were jumping from her eyes.

"And you don't get how to be normal!"

"Fine!"

"Whatever!"

"I'm not even talking to you anymore!"

"Me either."

"Good."

"Thought you said you weren't talking to me —"

"Oh, so did you!"

And you know we didn't, all the way back to the shop, where we found Darcelle standing outside with her arms folded. She wasn't happy either.

"*Mmmm-hmm*," she said, nodding her head up and down at me.

"Darcelle, I'm sorry, we were just passing by this really cool costume shop and —"

"And you think I don't know where Amazing Frank's is?" She turned, took two steps up the sidewalk, then turned again. "You think I don't know that you were obviously planning this all along? If you do, then you must also think I was born yesterday."

"I'm sorry."

"You better be. Let's go."

We didn't talk until back in the car.

"We were just getting —" Me — trying to make an excuse.

But Darcelle just cut me off. "I don't care what you got." She slammed the horn at a truck in front of us that was parked in the middle of the street. "*Mmm-hmm*, thought I could trust you . . ."

We were silent all the way home. Sara got out without a word. Darcelle dropped me off without a word.

If my parents hadn't been out at the store I don't know what would have happened. At least I got to hide the costume stuff, but I still figured Darcelle would be calling later to talk to Mom about what I had done. And you know, when she didn't, I only felt worse.

## CHAPTER 8
# A Sinking Feeling at the Tubs

If you are ever planning something big, you need to understand that it just doesn't matter how well things are going until one week before, because if things are going to fall apart, that's when it will start to happen. Of course, things were already falling apart for me — mad at my best friend, my stepsister mad at me, and having my mixed-up feelings about Carlos and the trick. But starting Monday afternoon, one week before we had to present our science projects and eight days before the trip, things got worse.

We were all at the Tubs trying to keep cool. Everything was fine, and Frankie was trying to tell us about aliens.

"D'you know that aliens, they come down and addup famous —"

"It's *abduct*." Thea — like she always did.

"Eeuuh, it's abduct!" Donte — like he always did, but only more ruthless since Thea punched him at the park last week.

And Thea glared at Donte like that might have to happen again.

"Yeah, anyway," Frankie kept going, "so the aliens, right, they come down and adduct famous singers and actors, like, all the time, right, like Elvis. . . ."

Frankie went on and on. Donte just sat all deep down in his tub. He had his black Raiders hat pulled down so far that you couldn't see anything above his scowl.

"Can we get back on track here, people?" Thea finally asked, sitting up in her tub again.

Me: "Sure."

Sara: "Fine."

Donte: "Guess."

Frankie: "A'ight. It's true, though, about the aliens."

And we all looked at Frankie, and nobody had to even say anything.

"So, we've got one week." Thea — getting down to

business. "And all I'm saying is I can't wait. Our spy visited the target's house, and now we have costumes. Trina, a report?"

"Sure," and I waited for a second so that Sara could huff, and you know she did.

I explained about going to Carlos's house, and how I got two costumes over the weekend.

"Ahem," Sara said, still not looking.

"Oh, right, *she* came along too."

"Nice job only getting two," Donte said, like he knew anything. "There are five of us, God!"

"Duh," Thea said. "Think about it, Donte. If all five of us are hiding out dressed as aliens, who is ever going to lead Carlos to where we are? And who is going to stay behind and make sure Ms. Atkinson doesn't suspect anything?"

Donte just mumbled to himself.

"What did you say?" Thea — starting to stand up. "I didn't hear you."

"Nothin'."

"That's what I thought." She sat back down.

I laughed and made sure it was loud enough for Donte to hear. Every time I looked at him, all I could think of was him on the jungle gym being so mean.

"So," Thea continued, "two people in costumes, off

114

in a nice hidden place, two of us to lead Carlos up to that place, and one of us to watch out back at the camp."

"Guess that'll be the lame ankle," Donte cracked.

"What?" Sara — suddenly looking up with her face all getting red.

"What's the matter, Sara?" Me — pouncing like I'd been waiting all day to say this. "Too busy reading your oh-so-important books?" Even as I said it, I could feel my hands starting to shake. Saying something nasty is hard work! I don't know how Thea and Donte do it all the time.

And the way Sara looked at me, well, you wouldn't even believe it, or what she said:

"Bitch."

"*Ohh!*" Frankie shouted, pumping his fist in the air.

"Let's go!" Donte — sitting up and knocking his hat back on his head. "Catfight!"

But there wasn't going to be any of that. Sara looked at me like she was trying to burn me with her eyes. I shook my head and smiled back at her. Served her right, thinking she was so much better than us. She looked back down in her lap, and I could see her starting to cry.

But then I wanted to cry too, 'cause this was all horrible, but there was no way I was giving in. Instead I quickly looked back over at Thea, who was arguing with Donte now about who would wear the costumes.

"It should be me and Frankie," Donte was saying, " 'cause girls are, like —"

"Smarter is what they are," Thea jumped in, "so don't even go there, Donte. You two would just end up getting silly and, like, farting on each other instead of doing your job."

"Whatever! What do you know?"

"I know how boys act," Thea kept on, and you could just feel it now between Thea and Donte. It was as bad as between Sara and me. "You and Frankie need to have the most serious job, the one that doesn't give you a chance to act like retards."

"Eeuh! You're a retard!" Donte snapped, with extra anger like I'd never heard before. "And, like, who wants to be part of your stupid plan when you don't even trust us?"

"Well, then maybe you shouldn't be a part of it!" Thea — standing up again.

Listening to them, my heart suddenly started racing in a different direction. What if this was it? What if the whole trick fell apart right here? We were all annoyed enough. Silently, I felt myself start rooting for more anger, maybe even a fight, to end all this.

But right then, the fence started to rattle and the subway came rumbling past, and we all stopped talking. White, hazy sunlight bounced off its silver roof and burned green spots into our eyes. I wondered if anyone saw us, and if we looked like the dirty city kids that we were being.

The train passed and the rumble on the tracks faded to a lower pitch, the way the sound of something does when it's leaving you. Now you could hear a couple birds in the trees on either side of the warehouse, even though you didn't notice them before.

Frankie suddenly spoke up, trying to change the subject again. "Sometimes aliens like to capture planes and take them into their ships and —"

"Oh my God." Donte lurched up to his feet. He jumped out of his tub and grabbed his empty bag by its long handle. "I'm outta here."

And just like that, he left.

Thea sat back down, trying to smile like nothing had happened. "So, where were we?"

But I was watching Donte leave. I was still the only one who knew that he was going to St. Anthony's. Maybe he was freaking out about that, and that's why he was being so nasty to people. But you know, knowing that only made me *more* mad at him, 'cause, like, why didn't he just tell people what was really bothering him, instead of being such a jerk? Then again, why wasn't I telling anyone about how this trick was secretly bothering me? I guess he wasn't ready, and neither was I.

"Hello, people?" Thea kept saying. "Don't worry about that idiot."

"Um," Frankie started, and when I looked over at him I saw that he was twisting his hat in his hands. "Maybe, like, now that Donte's gone, we should just forget about the plan. He's probably, like, just gonna tell on us anyway."

"Ha! He's still in on the plan, don't you worry," Thea said, "because if he wimps out he *knows what will happen.*"

"Still, man," Frankie went on, "this plan sounds boring."

And there it was. You just knew that when Frankie called something boring, what he really meant was one of two things: Either he didn't understand it or he was scared that he was going to get in trouble. I felt that secret hope again. Maybe if Frankie didn't want to do the trick either, then we wouldn't.

But Thea wasn't about to let that happen. "Boring? What's boring about it?"

I looked at Frankie not looking back at Thea. Then suddenly Sara spoke up:

"And why are *you* afraid of getting in trouble?" She stared at Frankie. Her eyes were still red.

"I'm not, it's just —"

"You get in trouble all the time!" Sara said coldly, her eyes glaring. "This shouldn't be a big deal for you, Frankie. You should have, like, fifty checks next to your name already!"

"So?" Frankie scowled. "Shut up."

"So . . ." Sara — not shutting up. "*You're* not the one who should be worried about getting in trouble."

Frankie waved his hat at her. "You always think you're better than everyone else —"

I just had to throw a nice little laugh out when Frankie said that, but it didn't make me feel any better. I mean, listen to us: Things were falling apart.

"Shoot," Frankie spat. "Me, I got important stuff too!"

"Oh right, like what?" Sara had tears on her cheeks.

"Like Walker Camp this summer!"

"What's that for, like —"

But now Thea cut Sara off: "For only, like, the best basketball players in Boston. No way, Frankie, you really got into Walker Camp?"

And the way Frankie smiled — you almost never see that smile on him. "And my aunt said that if I want to go, I gotta graduate to eighth grade, and I can't get in any more trouble."

And I figured that would be it for the trick. Walker Camp was something even Thea respected — but then I saw her at her best, or worst, making everything fit together and work for her.

"Frankie," she said, sounding like a teacher, "don't worry, we're not gonna let anything happen to mess that up. But you can't go to Walker Camp without some attitude, right? I mean, you know the best players are feared, because they're bad. You can't go all Goody Two-shoes or it'll make your game soft. You gotta be like Iverson, right?"

Frankie's eyes lit up. "Well, yeah . . . 'Cause Iverson, you know he's on the cops' hit list, but they can't touch him."

And Thea turned toward me and Sara and said, "It's like that for all of us, like we always say: You have to be a little bad sometimes, right?"

I looked over at Sara. This was one of those times when we would probably look at each other and be thinking the same thing, but she wasn't looking back. I felt dumb for even trying.

"Right," Sara said, getting her things together in her tub.

"Trina?" Thea was looking at me now.

Watching Thea flip Frankie's excuse right around into yet another reason why this trick was the right thing to do, I knew that no excuse I could make would work. I could try to explain how ever since I'd gone to Carlos's house, I'd been feeling like maybe we shouldn't do this, like maybe Carlos didn't deserve it. But Thea would turn that argument around in no time, or worse, I'd be the laughingstock of the seventh grade for *liking* Carlos. Thea could make that rumor happen, and at this point, Sara and Frankie would probably help her.

"Right," I said with a sigh, and my insides burned.

"I gotta go." Sara struggled to get out of her tub, then left without even looking over.

I wanted to run after her and say I was sorry for being so mean, but then I thought about how she was mean and she deserved it, and then I thought about how that didn't matter and what mattered was that I hated feeling like we weren't friends — but maybe I wasn't the one who needed to apologize first, because after all, she was the one who had changed and said all that stuff about being too important — or maybe this was all dumb, because we were best friends —

And by then it was too late. Sara was gone. Now Frankie and Thea were getting up to go too.

So we left the Tubs for the last time before our trip to New Hampshire. We walked along the trail beside the sound barrier, through steamy shade where the sun made leopard spots through the leaves. Frankie and Thea talked about Walker Camp. I walked alone behind them, feeling like a little gazelle, weakest of the herd, scanning the treetops for predators.

# CHAPTER 9
# The Rooftop World

A nd then it was Tuesday, officially one week before the trip, and I felt worse than ever. I couldn't get all that arguing from the Tubs out of my head. Sara and I not speaking, Donte storming off, Frankie getting cold feet, Thea turning it all around on him — it was too much. All morning, I couldn't concentrate on anything. And what did I have to look forward to at the end of the day? Another trip to Carlos's house.

And since none of my friends were really speaking to each other, I ended up spending the whole morning watching Carlos. He was in school on time and had been normal the whole week since my last visit. It was almost weird. Every time I looked at him, he was doing something all busily by himself that had nothing to do with whatever we were supposed to be doing.

Like in art, where we were working on these papier-mâché masks. Let me just say, I love art. As Ms. Romero, the art teacher, says: I've *"got it."* At least that's what she says whenever she's walking around telling everyone how to do the assignment and she gets to me and I'm already half done. I do really neat work, and when it comes to glitter or sequins, or any other sparkly design-making thing, you better just get ready. So my mask was looking good. Definitely better than Sara's.

Carlos, on the other hand, wasn't even working on his mask. Instead he was busy making tiny people out of a little ball of clay that he'd found who-knows-where. He had, like, ten of them standing on the newspaper in front of him. Everything Carlos made in art was small. Ms. Romero would give us, like, this big piece of watercolor paper, and Carlos would always draw all small and down in one corner. Ms. Romero was always asking him to "fill the page," because she said his drawings were good. So then he would keep working down in that tiny corner, and then right at the end of class he would write his name really really big across the rest of the paper. He worked on his little army for the whole time, never even touching his little mask.

Then in English, not my favorite class by the way: I mean, I love to write, and I love to read too, but that doesn't mean I like to write *about* reading — 'cause nothing ruins the fun of reading a good story like the evil English army of *Discuss, Analyze,* and that hideous duo *Compare and Contrast.* So anyway, we were all discussing what the red fern represented in that story about the two dogs that is so sad there is just no point in reading it, but Carlos had his head down in his book and was busy doodling in it, for, like, the whole time. It made sense to me now why, like, almost every time we finished a book and had to turn it in, Carlos would say he lost his.

At lunch, when all you were supposed to be doing was eating, Carlos was sitting by himself, not touching his little aluminum tray of nasty school lunch, and staring out the window. You might think that Carlos looked lonely, but he didn't. Still, I had this embarrassing urge to go talk to him. I sort of wanted to know what he was thinking about. Would he lie to me about aliens or what? And what was his little army in art for? And what did he draw in his English book? Stupid curiosity!

Plus, talking to Carlos sounded better to me than talking to any of my so-called friends. Thea was eating with some of the other girls, and I could hear them being all annoying and talking about videos and what the high-school boys that they were always pretending to know were up to. Donte and Frankie were sitting in the middle of a crowd of boys playing *Night of the Mutant Zombies XIV* and being all annoying and loud. Sara wasn't there because she had *oh-so-special* math lunch with Ms. Williams.

And I was sitting alone at a table, eating my ham sandwich and my Heavyn Bar, and even the Queen of Soul Candy couldn't improve my mood.

So by the time the end of the day came, I found myself actually maybe wanting to go to Carlos's house. But on the way, I just kept getting in a bad mood thinking about my annoying friends.

First there was Sara. What if school ended and we hadn't made up? Then the whole summer would go by. And in the fall, it always took a couple days of list-making to get us back on the same page. But what if there wouldn't be any list-making because we weren't friends anymore? Like, if we didn't fix our friendship now, would it be too late?

Next was Donte. Like, what if after these last two

weeks, I never even *saw* Donte again? On the one hand, I tried to think "good riddance" to him, he'd been such a big jerk lately, but stupid me, I still felt like I'd miss him. I'd known him since we were too small to remember, and it was just weird to think of him not being around.

Third, there was Frankie going to a basketball camp in the summer. Now he was like Sara with her swimming, and then there was boring old me. I didn't do anything. Shouldn't I have a special camp to go to?

And fourth, there was Thea and the trick. We all couldn't even get along with ourselves, how were we going to work together on the trick? And what about the fact that I didn't really want to do it, and yet I still wasn't saying anything about it? Was I a jerk for secretly hoping for more fighting between my friends, just so that the trick might not happen? How was that any better than planning a trick on Carlos?

My thoughts felt heavy like the humid, steamy air that was making my clothes all sticky and my socks all gross and wet. I was a selfish, evil person, wishing ill for my friends, and at the same time, feeling bad for the most annoying, weird boy in school.

And it was like the world agreed that every list should have five things, even my bad mood, because as soon as I turned the corner onto Carlos's street, I heard:

"Hey, there's Carlos's girl!"

"Uh-oh, heads up, y'all!"

It was a sunny, hazy day, but there might as well have been a rain cloud over my head.

This time the boys on Carlos's street were playing a basketball game, where the hoop was a red milk crate tied to a parking sign.

"Girl, you sure you want to be with him? 'Cause you could be with me!"

I walked past with my head down, slammed through Carlos's front gate, stomped up the stairs, and rang the bell.

Bass was booming from the second floor again, a really intense Caribbean downbeat. Now I heard Carlos's little feet coming down the stairs, and then a loud banging like he tripped or something, which turned out to be what had happened, 'cause when he opened the door, he was wincing and rubbing at his elbow.

"Heyyy," he said in his tiny voice.

I rolled my eyes. "What happened to you?"

"I tripped, it's nothing."

I just huffed. "Let's just get upstairs already."

"Roger."

I followed him upstairs, past the thumping bass on the second floor, past Kasey with her black hair all frizzed out this way and that and wearing a pink nightshirt even though it was, like, the middle of the afternoon, past Alexis on the phone with the TV blaring, and past the kitchen that reeked like old pizza.

"Sorry about the mess in here," Carlos said as we walked into his room, and when I looked around, I almost just turned and walked right out.

There were clothes everywhere, practically covering the floor, and you have to understand that a lot of it was underwear. Not just little pink-and-blue Kasey underwear with, like, rabbits and dolls on it, but white Carlos underwear too. I'm serious.

"Oh my God! Gross!" Me — shaking my head, because I'm not even talking about, like, boxers, which would be gross enough, thank you very much, I'm talking about *briefs*. Tight, white, boys' underwear with the elastic band around the waist with the two blue stripes.

"It's all clean, I swear!" Carlos said, kicking a pair off the yellow beanbag and sitting down. "It's just that I have to fold it and put it away. Sorry."

"Sorry? I can't believe you brought me in your room with all your nasty underwear!" I waited until he had cleared off the bed, then sat down.

Carlos piled all the clothes together on the floor. "Oh," he said like he remembered something, then ducked down in that space between the two beds. He pulled a wrinkled piece of white notebook paper out from underneath the pile of clothes he'd just made.

"Please tell me those are your notes from watching the video."

"Yeah." He sat back on the beanbag.

"Let me see."

"They're not very good," he said, not handing them to me. "The first time I watched it, I just got too bored, but the second time I was able to get some stuff." He handed them over.

I looked at the beat-up paper. At first, I couldn't even see the notes at all. The paper was covered with drawings in black marker. Across the top there was a line of mountains, and the center one had a tower on the top. Below that, the paper was covered with symbols, like strange Greek-looking things. The one that he'd drawn over and over was a circle with an $x$ across it. There was a dot in each of the four pie pieces that the $x$ made. It looked like this:

And there were all these other rough, squiggly lines winding in between the symbols and mountains, and I had already huffed and was about to give up completely when I realized that these lines were actually made of words. These were Carlos's notes about the video. I had to turn the paper like a steering wheel, around and around just to read the first one:

*Lions will make dens on hi rocks where they ken watch over there prey.*

"Why don't we let me do the writing for the report?" I said, calming down now just a little. "You can do the drawings for the presentation."

"But —"

"But what?"

"Well," Carlos said, "what if I don't finish them? Sometimes I get distracted. . . ."

"But you won't because you're not going to have any Day Afters or anything between now and the trip, right?"

"Well —"

"No. None, Carlos. It better not happen."

"Roger."

We both sat there for a minute. Bass from downstairs vibrated the floor on every downbeat. I looked down at Carlos's notes. "What are all these drawings of?"

"Oh!" Carlos looked up at me like he'd just seen me for the first time or something. "Those are pictures of what I think the trip will look like. I can't wait to go!"

"Sure, well, that's good. It, um, should be fun," I said, feeling a little guilty wave.

"I love hiking," Carlos was saying. "And mountains." He gazed out the window.

Sitting there on the floor, he looked so small. I took a deep breath and reached into my bag. "Look," I said, handing him a stack of note cards, "I copied my notes from reading that book. You can draw big posters of each of our main animals and put the important facts on the back, okay?"

Carlos took the cards, barely looking at them. "Okay."

I looked around Carlos's room, and all those drawings on his wall caught my eye. Many of them were of mountains, and now I saw that that symbol from his notes, the circle with the $x$ and the dots, was on every drawing: in the corners, on houses, on the chests of superheroes.

"Carlos, your drawings are kind of good." I pointed to the walls. "Are all these of the trip too?" I asked.

"What?" He looked around, then suddenly jumped up. "Oh!" Carlos shook his head like he was snapping back to reality again. "No, most of them are from — yeah! This is totally what I wanted to show you last time too!" He ran over to the window and started yanking it open. "Out here."

"Out?"

He gritted his teeth. "Yeah." He struggled to lift the squealing window.

"No way."

"No, come on, it's — really — cool!" The window shot open. "No aliens, I swear."

I sucked my teeth at him, but then I got up and walked toward the window. For the first time all day, I forgot about all the problems I had with every-one I knew. The little kid was climbing right out his window and you know that I was just too curious again.

Carlos's head popped back in. "You have to kinda hurry, so Alexis doesn't notice."

I followed him out onto a small ledge made by this little roof over a large, rounded window in the apartment below. Carlos leaned off the edge and grabbed onto a black metal fire-escape ladder. He swung over and started climbing.

I walked across the narrow green slate ledge and stretched to reach the ladder. If Carlos could do it with those little arms of his, then so could I, but the reach was a little farther than I thought. I grabbed it and for a second I froze, holding the ladder but with my feet still on the little roof. There was a window right next to me. All Alexis or Kasey had to do was turn around and they would see me, no problem. Then I looked down at the narrow strip of shade and dirt between Carlos's house and the red house next door, and all I could see were rocks and a fence and my stabbed and bleeding body lying there after I fell.

"Hurry up!" Carlos called. I looked up and saw his head sticking out from over the roof, in between the curved sides of the ladder's end.

I held my breath, leaned out, and swung my feet over. My pants caught on the side of the ladder for just a second but came free when I started climbing.

The ladder led to the flat roof of Carlos's three-family house. It was an uneven patchwork of tar squares, dotted with puddles and all kinds of rusted junk: cans, aluminum dinner trays, and a huge TV antenna that was lying dead like a fallen tree across the middle of the roof. The puddles were steaming in the high, white-hot sun, and waves of heat shimmered off the squares of black tar like they would melt your shoes right down to your feet, and then your skin after that.

Carlos was climbing through the giant antenna, toward the far side of the roof. He looked back at me and waved his hand: "Come on!"

I have to admit: It was cool up there. But I wasn't climbing through some big nasty antenna, when you could just walk around the back of it instead. On the other side, there was a big mess of rusty cans and moldy plastic bottles. It wasn't until I was about to kick through them that I realized they were arranged in that same circle-and-$x$ symbol from Carlos's drawings. I actually looked up at the sky for a second before I remembered, duh, there weren't *really* any aliens visiting Carlos. But this was different than talking about aliens in school. If he was making signs for them on his roof where no one could see . . . It made me wonder if maybe Carlos hoped aliens would come — maybe he wished his problems really were because of aliens. My brain was buzzing now with all these thoughts.

I found Carlos sitting over on the far side of the roof, next to three little satellite TV dishes, with his legs dangling over the edge, his bare heels kicking against the brown side of the house.

"You're crazy. You're gonna fall."

"Nah, I sit here all the time. Look."

He pointed out across a checkerboard of silver and black roofs that seemed to never end. It almost looked like you could hop from one to the next. And sticking up from them like teeth were all kinds of antennas, bent chimneys, skylights, big old satellite dishes and the smaller, plate-sized ones. A roof to the left had a square of picket fence with a garden inside it. Another had a cheap-looking greenhouse made of wood beams and sheets of plastic, but you could tell that there was, like, a tiny steaming jungle inside it by the big leafy prints pushing up against the sides. Another had a deck like you'd see on the back of a house, but stuck right up on the roof, with lounge chairs and a plastic table with a blue-and-green-striped umbrella. Another roof had a big white woman in a pink bikini out sunbathing and almost blinding us with her bare skin. One had a basketball hoop standing in the middle. A frayed old couch, a purple tent, grass, flow-ers, gas grills, a broken dishwasher, bowling pins, an easel, a telescope, a hammock between two chimneys —

It was like a whole separate city. I was imagining bridges between each roof, a world where people never had to go down to the dirty streets.

"Cool, huh?" Carlos said.

"Yeah," I said, 'cause it was. "I can't believe how much junk people have on their roofs." I sat down beside him, putting one leg over the side, but keeping the other one in.

"Not that," Carlos said, like I was missing the point, and he pointed way off into the hazy heat, past the rooftops, to where you could just see the ant-sized cars bouncing the sunlight around on the highway, and beyond to where a line of low green hills, called the Blue Hills because of why-I-have-no-idea, rose up above everything.

"You mean *those*?" I had been there a bunch of times, and while they weren't as boring as, say, what passed for a beach in Boston, they were pretty boring if you compared them to any kind of real mountains, like the pictures I'd seen of the Rockies. As I was looking at them now, though, I did notice that on the one on the far right, called Big Blue, you could see the weather observatory on top, which was probably what Carlos had drawn on his notes.

"So this is what your drawings were of."

"I guess." He kept staring out that way.

"I'll give you this, Carlos, it's pretty neat up here. I like the rooftops. I bet you see a lot of people doing strange things."

"Huh? People?"

"Yeah, like that whale over there sunbathing." And I had to point because Carlos didn't even know what I was talking about. I couldn't believe that he hadn't noticed.

"Well," he said, "yeah."

We sat there quiet for a second, and I could hear those sounds, like the basketball game, and the bass from downstairs, and air conditioners and all — sounds from the real world that you weren't a part of up here.

"Mostly I like to imagine what's up there," he said, pointing to Big Blue and still smacking his heels against the brown wood.

"Yeah, you'd have to imagine, right? I mean, 'cause there's really nothing that interesting up there, don't you remember? We did that hike up there in fifth grade, to the weather observatory at the top —"

"That's what that thing is?"

"Duh, Carlos. Why do you sound surprised? We spent, like, two hours in there."

"I didn't get to go on that field trip."

"Oh. Well, you would have liked it up there."

"Really? What was it like?" Carlos slid closer to me.

"What, the hike or the observatory?" I said, sliding a little farther away.

"Both."

"Well, the hike was kind of cool because there were big rocks along the trail, and sometimes they were slippery —"

"Did you fall?"

"No, but this one time Donte did and that was worth the whole trip. Anyway, when you got about halfway up, then you got out of the trees for a minute and you could look back on all of Boston, and it was kind of like looking out on a foreign city, you know? Like you were an explorer and you'd discovered it, with its shining towers and stuff —"

"Cool."

"Of course it was cool, but stop interrupting me already. So then —"

"Sorry."

"Uh! Do you have anything else to say before I start again?"

"Um . . . what was the top like?"

"That's what I'm trying to tell you about!"

"Okay." Carlos smiled.

And you know, for the first time all day, I smiled too.

"So, at the top there are all these fields, and it's cool because you can see where this big fire burned all the trees, and they're all black and charred, but then the grass is new and green.

"And the weather observatory is this old, round little castle, from, like, the eighteen hundreds or something, and it's full of all these machines that are from, like, the nineteen seventies. And they don't have cool screens or games or anything, they're just scribbling lines on graph paper that are supposed to tell the weather. But the roof of the observatory is cool, because there are all these instruments that are actually measuring stuff you could see and feel."

I looked down and the way little Carlos was looking back up at me made me feel like it must have felt to be Thea, when she was thinking up a new plan at the Tubs, or Sara when she was getting ready to race. Granted, the Carlos spotlight wasn't exactly as big as the four-friends spotlight, or the pool-club spotlight, but it felt warm like the sun.

"The best one," I kept on explaining, "was this thing called a, uh, oh yeah, check this out: It was called a pyroheliometer. It was this glass ball, like the size of one of those candlepin bowling balls over at Boston Bowl —"

"Yeah, I like those —"

"Oh my God, will you stop interrupting!" I snapped, but I was smiling.

"Roger." Carlos smiled too.

"Anyway, so it was this glass ball, right, and it was held by these two metal fingers, like this —" I pointed my right index finger up and my left one down at it with a space in between. "The sun would shine through the ball and onto a strip of paper, like, as wide as a ruler, underneath. So, whenever the sun was out, the glass ball would focus the light so that it would burn a mark into the paper like it was searing flesh."

By the way, I don't really know what burning flesh looks like, but it's always more interesting explaining something if you have good and gross comparisons.

"And since you know the sun moves across the sky all day, the burn mark goes across the paper, and if it was cloudy, there'd be a part of the paper with no burn, and then when the sun came back out it would be burned again. And they had this book, right, that had every one of these strips for the last hundred years, which sounds boring, but any science instrument that burns things is cool, right?"

"Yeah." Carlos gazed out at the hazy hills again.

"Sara and I were imagining how badly you could burn an ant if you — hey! Are you still listening?"

"Yeah, I am." He turned back to me. "It just all sounds so cool, like, being up there, on the top of that castle on top of the mountain, with that cool weather thing."

"It was. It was even cooler when Frankie was so scared of heights and didn't get off his hands and knees the whole time."

Suddenly Carlos frowned. "I hope I get to go on the trip."

"You —" I sighed. "Carlos, you have, like, two checks. Why wouldn't you get to go?"

"I don't know. You never know."

"But you *do* know, Carlos. No problems during the presentation, just like we said, and you'll be all set."

"Well, roger. But —" Carlos looked down and

watched his own kicking feet. "It would be easier without me. It's always easier without me. I always slow the class down, I'm slow getting ready in the morning . . . and I'll be a slow hiker, I know it. All the other boys will be annoyed with me and it'll be my fault we don't get to the top of the mountain."

I swallowed hard, and then I said, "Carlos, you're going to be fine on the trip." He smiled. My gut rumbled, but I felt like I meant it.

"I don't know. . . ."

"Well, listen," I heard myself saying. "First we'll ace this science presentation. And then you'll go on the trip and it'll be great. It'll make up for all the trips you've missed." As I said it, I thought: *At least if a few so-called friends don't play a trick on him, and how are you going to make that happen, Ms. Suddenly-oh-so-goody-goody?*

"Maybe . . ." Carlos looked at me like he trusted me. Like we were friends. And I wondered: Maybe we were.

Then he spun and dropped back onto the roof. "You should probably go now."

I shook my head. "Huh? Oh yeah, I guess so." I dropped down from the ledge.

"Thanks for coming up here with me. And for telling me about the pyro-thingy." Carlos was looking away, but he held out his hand. I shook it.

"Sure," I said and started walking back around the antenna. "Do those animal drawings, okay, and we'll work on the presentation when Mr. Fissile gives us time on Friday. Oh, and listen: When I leave this time, could you try not to yell —"

But when I turned around, Carlos was back sitting on the ledge, all small and looking out over the rooftop city, toward Big Blue, like I had left hours ago.

## CHAPTER 10
# Questioned by My So-called Friends

**S**o I wasn't going to do the trick.

How could I?

It wasn't just the guilt-demon anymore. It was worse:

It was me. I liked Carlos. Now, I don't mean I *liked* him, like I was suddenly going to start whispering about him from across the room and giggling, or tripping him or anything. I just mean that he was neat. He was nice. I think I cared about him, NOT in a gross way, just — like a friend, I guess. And wasn't I good for him? Wasn't it good for him to have someone to show his rooftop world to? What if being friends with me made his problems *better*?

So that was that. And luckily, the fact that I wasn't going to do the trick wasn't even going to come up because none of my *so-called friends* were speaking. Sara and I weren't talking. Donte and Thea weren't talking. I made sure to never be in the same place as Thea, and Frankie might as well have been abducted by aliens for how much he seemed to be around.

So I walked into school the next Monday, the day of the presentation and the day before the overnight, feeling pretty good.

And then the rest of Monday happened.

I got to Ms. Atkinson's class a few minutes early to check in with Carlos —

Only he wasn't there. Late. No way. It wasn't possible. Class started, and all I was doing was watching the door out of the corner of my eye. The minutes ticked by, and still no Carlos. He couldn't do this — he wouldn't — not on the day of our presentation. . . .

Then I saw it out of the corner of my eye: that little head in the doorway.

And his hair, it was —

Normal. Braided. Still, Carlos was sticking his head into the room like he would on a Day After.

"Oh," Ms. Atkinson said, turning from the chalkboard and suddenly grabbing on to the side of her desk

146

like she was bracing for the worst. "Good morning, Carlos."

"Good morning, Ms. Atkinson," Carlos said in a —

Totally normal voice. As he made his way to his seat I saw that he was tapping on a stack of large papers underneath his arm, and I knew they were our drawings. This was really going to be okay. Carlos sat down and didn't fall out of his chair. Relief washed away all my fears and I slouched down so far I almost fell under the table.

Then I looked back at him, just to make sure.

He smiled back.

And he was fine in art, where he made a tiny little painting, all small and in the bottom corner of his paper, just like usual. And in English — doodling just like every other wonderfully fantastically normal day.

By the time we got to lunch and things were still all nice and normal, I was beaming. I even stopped over by the table where Carlos was sitting with Dr. Johnson. He was going over some work while absolutely normally not touching his tin plate of school lunch. Dr. Johnson looked up at me, but Carlos was busy reading.

"Hello, Trina," she said, pushing her square glasses up.

"Hey."

"Carlos tells me you two have done a lot of work for this presentation."

"I guess." Carlos was still reading the back of a large paper in front of him, like we weren't even there.

"Well, he and I have been going over and over his work, so that he'll be prepared for this afternoon." She nodded at me.

"That's good." I turned to Carlos. "How are you?" He still didn't even notice.

Dr. Johnson nudged him.

He jumped. "What — me? Oh — hi, Trina. I'm fine."

"Carlos," Dr. Johnson said, "why don't you show Trina your drawings?"

"Oh yeah." He flipped over the stack of large papers and spread them out on the table. "They're all fin- ished and I only kinda messed up the hyena . . . see? It looks like a poodle."

"Now, Carlos," Dr. Johnson said, only Carlos was right: It did look like a poodle.

"Well," I said, "but it's the only doglike animal, so nobody will get it confused. Wow, Carlos." I picked up his leopard in a tree. "These are — big." I didn't want to say *great*, because they weren't, but they *filled the*

148

*page.* Each animal was outlined in black marker and then colored in all nice and neat with crayons.

"Thanks." Carlos smiled and looked away. "So . . . are you ready too?"

"Yeah. I'll do the intro for each animal, and then you can explain the important facts like we went over in class on Friday. You do know those, right?"

"Oh!" Carlos smacked himself in the forehead.

"Carlos —" Dr. Johnson started.

"No! I mean — yeah! Dr. J and I wrote them out this morning. See —" He picked up his lion drawing and flipped it over, not noticing as his sleeve rubbed right through that rusty pile of kitchen sponges they call barbeque chicken nuggets in the school lunch. "We taped them on the back, so I — so I can read them while I'm holding up each drawing."

"And we've gone over them many times," Dr. Johnson added, "haven't we?"

"Roger."

"So . . ." I nodded at Carlos. "We're all set."

"Yup."

"Nothing unexpected is going to go wrong or anything like that."

Carlos looked up at me, then sideways. "Not if I can help it."

"Now, Carlos." Dr. Johnson patted him on the shoulder. "We've talked about this, haven't we? There's nothing wrong with being nervous about the presentation" — she was saying it half to him and half to me — "but that's no reason not to do your best, right?"

Carlos sighed. "Roger." He didn't smile.

"Good," I said, and reached over and play-punched him on the arm. "See you in science, Carlos."

" 'Kay."

I walked away and was just about to let out a smile when I heard from beside me:

"What, are you guys in *love* now, or something?"

I turned to find Donte, Thea, Frankie, and Sara all crowded together at the same table. I wrinkled my nose. "Shut up, Donte, like you have any idea what —"

But Thea cut me off. "Trina!" she hissed. "Sit down, quick!" She kicked out the chair beside her.

I looked at it and thought, *You should just walk away, say you have a question for Ms. Atkinson, anything* — Right then and there, I could just say no and turn solo. Like Heavyn at the Grammys when she announced she was leaving the Divine Divas. Except

150

she'd done that right in the middle of their Best Album acceptance speech in front of thousands, which was kind of like if I were to tell my *so-called friends* that I was done with them right here in the lunchroom. I'd hear it from the crowd just like she did.

"Come on already!" Frankie whined.

So I sat down, only to find them all staring at me, like I was a captured double agent and now it was time for the torture. I just shrugged my shoulders. "What?"

"So," Thea said, "you're still in, right?"

I tried to change the subject. "Thea, why are you sitting next to Donte?"

She looked at me like I was mental. "What? We're friends."

"Duh," Donte added at me.

"But what about last week? You guys were fighting, and —"

Thea rolled her eyes like that was the most obvious thing in the world. "That was last week. Besides, there are more important things to worry about *this* week, right?"

"Well." I could feel my heart racing, trying to break out and run. "Yeah —"

"And you're still in for *those things,* right?"

"Well . . ." I stuttered, trying to smile, "yeah, I mean — of course, why are you even asking —"

"We have our reasons to be suspicious," Sara muttered.

I tried to look shocked, when really, I felt naked. "What are you talking about?"

"We see how you are with Carlos," Thea said.

"How I —"

"Yeah, it's all gross." Donte — making his school-lunch face again. "It's like you *like* him."

"Oh my God, I do not!" I could feel myself starting to sweat now.

"See?" Sara said to Thea, like I wasn't even there or something. "I told you she'd try to deny it. I don't think we can trust her."

"You —" I pushed back from the table and stood up. "I'm not listening to this," I said, hating how guilty I sounded.

"So . . ." Thea crossed her arms, her face all stern. "That's it, then? You're out?"

"I —"

Donte shook his head. "Letting down your best friends —"

"Shut up!" I hissed, like I was too stupid to say

anything else. Then I pointed at Frankie. "What about *him*? Last week he was all wanting to end the trick so he wouldn't get in trouble!"

"Don't point at me." Frankie — shaking his head. "I never said that."

"You totally did, Frankie, and don't lie 'cause you *know what will happen!*"

"Well, if I said it, I didn't mean it," Frankie said. "*I'm* not letting down my best friends."

"We know," said Donte, patting him on the shoulder. "We know *you're* okay, Frankie."

"Yeah." Thea nodded. "We know *you* wouldn't diss us."

And then they all looked back at me.

I had to tell them, right then. How I really felt. I had to look at my *so-called friends* and just tell them I was out. *This trick is stupid and Carlos doesn't deserve it.* That was all I had to say.

But then I realized that wasn't going to work. If I was out, they would just do it without me, wouldn't they? And that wasn't going to do Carlos any good. I realized that I didn't just not want to do the trick, I didn't want the trick to be done.

So I had to make them understand. I had to make them see about Carlos. He was annoying, but not because he wanted attention. That was the *last* thing he wanted. And lately, he'd been better. I needed them to see that maybe someone being nice to him was doing more than some silly trick ever could. Had he had a Day After since we'd started working together? Had he stolen anything or even made a single weird noise?

But there was no way to explain this to my *so-called friends*. I just knew it. They needed to see for themselves. And that's when I realized that they would, this afternoon, when Carlos and I did our presentation perfectly.

They would see, and then they would know what I knew: that the best thing we could do was *not* play this trick. The best thing we could do was just let Trina keep working her magic. After they saw the presentation, *then* I could talk to them, and they'd get it.

And so that's why I said: "Fine, all right, fine! I'm in! Can I go eat now already?"

"What's stopping you?" Sara whispered.

"Ugh!"

As I walked off, I heard Donte, hamming it up like he was so funny: "I don't know, are you sure we can trust her?"

And when I sat back down at my seat I was still so mad. As I tore open my Heavyn bar, do you know who I was absolutely the most mad at, out of all of them?

That's right — Sara. It was one thing for Donte or Thea to act like they always did, but for Sara to go along with them, when of all of us, this whole trick was the least like her — or at least, the her I used to know — I could have told *that* Sara about all the good things that happened with Carlos, but not this one. She was just another *so-called friend*.

Lunch lasted ten more endless minutes. I sat by myself and started to worry. What if they didn't see? What if the perfect presentation wasn't enough? Then I would have to choose between them and Carlos.

Could I make that choice? Hopefully, after science class, I wouldn't have to.

# CHAPTER 11
# The Presentation

Carlos and I were the sixth group to go, right in the middle. Sara and Frankie went fourth. They had a long timeline, obviously made by Sara, that covered the whole chalkboard and explained the history of alien sightings and abductions, starting all the way back in the times of ancient Native Americans.

"The early Anasazi people of North America are thought to have been abducted by aliens," Ms. Oh-So-Important went on and on, "because the archaeological evidence shows that one day they were here, and then one day they were just gone. . . ." All Frankie did was hold up this, like, four-foot-tall painting of an ugly green alien with arrows and explanations of different alien features, like big brains for mind control and big eyes for hypnosis and seeing underwater.

And Sara talked and talked. God! If Mr. Fissile hadn't made it a rule that any heckling would make your group lose points, I would have been coughing and dropping pennies on the floor, just to disturb *Queen Know-it-all*. Luckily, the presentations had a time limit, or she would have gone on all day.

I kept looking back to the table where Carlos was sitting, checking to make sure nothing strange was starting to happen. Still, with only one group before us, he seemed normal. Dr. Johnson was sitting beside him, flipping through his drawings so that he could sneak looks at the facts on the back. I was doing the same thing with my pile of cards in my lap.

And our report was going to be better than Sara's, or at least more scientific. I mean, alien mind control? Please. Although I knew she probably had her mom, the lawyer, read her paper and make sure it was perfect so she would get the best grade anyway, like she so annoyingly always did. But it didn't matter, because our report was really about Carlos and me. They would see. They would all see.

The fifth team to go was Caitlin and Shawn, and their report was about volcanoes. Caitlin had her hair all done up in big curls, like this was a dance or something. Shawn had on a tie, and he looked *fine*, but you know that was Caitlin's doing. They had a model volcano that was, like, three feet tall and all made of papier-mâché and painted just like a mountain, and everything was going fine until it was time to make the model erupt using vinegar and baking soda.

Caitlin kept sounding out words, like we were in kindergarten and she was the teacher. "We're going to sim-u-late lava by mixing vinegar and baking soda, just like Mr. Fissile taught us way back." And you know she flashed her wide, Caitlin kissing-up smile over at Mr. Fissile, who tried to smile back but was too busy suddenly rubbing at his hairy chin, probably remembering that time back in fifth grade when this girl Penny had dumped a gallon of vinegar in his fish tank, killing his giant Amazon Paku fish.

"I'm adding a few drops of food coloring," Caitlin went on, "to make the mix-ture look more like lava." You could tell that if she sounded out one more word, everyone was going to heckle her to death, grades or not. But then she was pouring the vinegar into the top of the volcano.

For just a second, nothing happened, and Maurice even had time to say, "Boring —"

And then suddenly, foamy red lava started bubbling out of the top with a wet hiss and flowing down the sides of the model. We all nodded and mumbled with approval. Then we shouted with approval as the lava rinsed all the brown and green paint right off the sides of the volcano, and the reddish, guts-colored goo started running all over the lab table and spilling down onto the tile floor. Caitlin hadn't noticed yet and kept pouring more vinegar into the foam-spitting volcano, but Shawn — he was out of there, and Mr. Fissile was running over.

He was all, "Okay, okay, Caitlin, we get it, that's um, great, and . . ." Caitlin stepped back and we all held our breath hoping she would slip, and you could hear everyone exhale, disappointed, when she didn't.

Mr. Fissile looked down at the soaked and gooey floor and shook his head. "Well, Caitlin, Shawn, nice job. Way to bring the natural disaster right into the classroom." He moved the wet, flopping volcano model down to the floor behind the counter, then wiped off the table as best he could, but it was still slimy and gross. "Everybody be careful up here," he said, checking his watch and grabbing a roll of paper towels. "Just walk on the paper towels; we're in a bit of a rush to get these done." He started dropping long lengths onto the floor. Ms. Atkinson came over from the side of the room, where she was probably watching Mr. Fissile more than our presentations, and helped wipe up. Mr. Fissile said, "Next we have Trina and Carlos."

"Tweedo!" Maurice blurted from the back corner of the room, earning himself a school-record thirty-third check.

As I headed to the front of the room, I checked my white button-down shirt and khaki dress-code pants. Everything was in order. I ran a hand back over my braids, just to make sure nothing was sticking out funny. As I stepped up to the front table, I heard the splat of my tall black clogs in the sticky soup of red vinegar, paint, and paper towels on the floor. The table was soaked, so I kept my distance. Then I looked for *him*.

And Carlos was on his way to the front of the room. Dr. Johnson stood and patted his shoulder as he headed slowly toward me — looking normal — nervous, but still normal. He had his drawings under his arm and was watching his feet carefully, like he didn't trust them.

"*Tweedo loco!*" Donte called out as Carlos passed him. Dr. Johnson shushed him, but snickers still snuck around the room like thieves.

"Be careful of the floor," Mr. Fissile warned.

"O-okay," Carlos croaked.

He came around to my left, almost stepping right into the volcano, but managed to kind of hop, kind of fall over it. He landed on his feet, but another snicker broke loose. Finally Carlos stood up next to me and put his drawings down.

"No, don't — " I hissed — but he dropped them right onto the still-slimy table.

"O-oh . . ." He grabbed the pictures and wiped at the bottom of the pile, sending a spray of red vinegar onto his white shirt.

"Problems!" Maurice blurted out for check number thirty-four.

"All right, Maurice." Ms. Atkinson was by his chair in a second. "Let's go . . . out." She led him out of the room.

"Sorry about that," Mr. Fissile said to us. "Carlos, why don't I hold those for you?" He took a step toward us.

I could feel my face getting red. My hands were starting to shake.

"That's okay," Carlos said, holding up the drawings in front of him.

Dr. Johnson was halfway up the aisle. "Carlos?"

But he straightened his shoulders and nodded. "I've got it."

Then he looked up at me, his eyes all big, like I might say something helpful, like a friend. So I did. "We'll be fine," I whispered, and as I said this I nodded my head up and down real slow, to let Carlos know that we *had* to be fine.

I looked back out at the room, and I could feel all the eyes like spotlights on me. I saw Frankie looking at me like he was thinking about shooting free throws, Sara glaring at me like she hoped I'd mess up, Donte grinning at me like he knew we would fail, and Thea whispering to her neighbor. Some friends. But we would show them.

So I started: "Our final project is about the five major predators of the Serengeti. We researched the lion, cheetah, leopard, hyena, and crocodile, and compared and contrasted their adaptations and hunting strategies." Now I could feel things settle in. I was talking, and I was good at it. I could handle the spotlights, and I could handle my partner, and I could handle my *so-called friends*.

"There are other vicious predators in the Serengeti, like scorpions and wild dogs, but we decided to keep it simple and only study the cool animals."

Out of the corner of my eye I could tell that Carlos was shaking a little beside me, but he was holding it together. He looked down at his drawings and every once in a while up at Dr. Johnson, who was standing at the back of the room and nodding. She made an up-and-down motion to him with her hand, like he should take a deep breath. I heard him suck in a gallon of air and blow it out.

"'Cause let's be honest," I continued, "when was the last time you saw a scorpion having, like, its own Disney movie?" The class even laughed a little. "The first animal we studied was the lion. Carlos?"

You know, you could just feel all the spotlights in the room turn —

And Carlos didn't say anything. He just stood there. Then he reached up and scratched at the left side of his head.

"Ahem," I said, a nervous bolt shooting through my gut.

Another second went by and still nothing. Dr.

Johnson took a step toward the front of the room, making that deep-breath motion with her hand again. This was it, he was going to lose it —

Carlos sucked in more air, then finally spoke. "Li-ions," he said too softly, then shook his head like he was returning from outer space. He flipped nervously through his drawings. He pulled out the lion, put it on top, and held it up for the class to see.

"Is that Lassie?" Donte called out.

"Donte!" Mr. Fissile snapped. "I warned you once. That'll be detention, a good time for me to call your mother." He slapped a check up on the board.

"Shoot," Donte muttered, probably more because that was his eighth check, so he knew he had to relax.

Mr. Fissile turned to us again. "Go ahead, Carlos."

But I already could see the problem here. Carlos had written the lion notes on the back of the lion drawing, but since he couldn't put the other drawings down on the wet counter, the lion was in front of the others, and so he was looking at notes for the wrong animal. He stood there with the drawings in front of his face, squinting at the list in front of him, knowing it didn't make sense. Finally, I reached over and snatched the other drawings from him.

"Oh yeah," Carlos sighed, and glanced over at me as I rolled my eyes with relief. *"Things that are interesting about lions."*

As Carlos began reading the list, I shot a little victory smirk right out at my friends. And I tilted my head at Carlos, like to say: *Ha.*

Carlos read fast, in, like, one breath: "Okay, so —

1. They have so much pride that they live in one.

2. Only the males have manes, and they think this makes them the best so they lie around being lazy all the time.

3. Female lions do all the work, and most of the hunting.

4. Sometimes when a new male takes over a pride, he will eat the babies of the old male, and that's REALLY GROSS.

5. Lions are stronger than the other big cats, but not as fast as the cheetah, and not as good as the leopard at climbing trees."

Carlos looked over at me, gasping for breath. I smiled, I couldn't help it. Everything was going to be all right.

I went on: "Lion prides are like big families, and much larger than the cheetah families. Cheetahs are more endangered than lions because even though they are faster, it is harder for them to keep what they catch —"

So, blah blah, I was going on and on, and it was going great, and so finally I said: "Now we'll discuss the leopard. Carlos?"

I turned to him —

And he was scratching. His stomach. On the outside of his shirt.

I froze. "Carlos."

He looked down at his stomach like he was surprised to see that he was scratching it. "Uh-oh," he moaned weakly.

I held the leopard drawing out to him. "Read the list!" I hissed.

He grabbed for it wildly and knocked it out of my hand. It fell right into the mess of paint and vinegar on the table. He got his shaking hands on it and lifted up the slippery, dripping paper.

"Come on!" I grunted, gritting my teeth.

"O-o-kay," he said, and you know my heart skipped a beat because he said it in *that voice.* "Thi-ings that are co-ol a-abo-ut leh-perds."

He started shaking all over.

Donte and the others started whispering and snickering, like hyenas who smelled a kill.

"Carlos, do you need a minute?" Mr. Fissile asked, stepping over from the side of the room.

"Carlos," I said, not even bothering to whisper now, "don't do this."

He let go of the drawing and suddenly yanked his shirt open to scratch at his stomach.

"I—I ca-an't he-lp i-i-it —"

"Yes, you can!" I hissed, my heart racing and my hands starting to sweat. Now Carlos dropped the leopard drawing back onto the wet table and started scratching with both hands so hard that his whole body shook.

"Carlos . . ." Dr. Johnson was rushing toward the front of the room. "Let's step outside."

"Problems!" Frankie shouted and the whole room cackled, circling, ready to eat.

"Frankie!" Mr. Fissile shouted, then he raised his

voice to the whole class like you never hear him do. "That's enough! You will not treat your classmate this way! All of you have been nervous before, and —"

I was barely paying attention, 'cause I was busy looking from the class to Carlos and back. "Come on, Carlos," I whispered, tears springing to my eyes.

Carlos barely glanced at me.

"Carlos, outside, right now . . ." Dr. Johnson was making her way around the front table.

"And you will listen to your classmate's presentation with respect and silence," Mr. Fissile was finishing, scaring the hyenas off, but by the time he turned back, it was too late.

Dr. Johnson was reaching for Carlos's arm —

And then everything happened at once, and I swear it was just like in the movies, with the slow motion that makes everyone's voices sound wrong and everything.

"A-aa-aah!" Carlos suddenly grabbed at his head and his braids started coming undone and his hair started shooting up straight and off to the left. His whole body started vibrating all out of control.

I reached for him — I don't know if I was going to try to help him, or if I was going to try to *make* him read the sopping-wet poster — stupid me still thought there was a chance — but when my hand touched his elbow he twisted away from me.

"Save yourself!" he yelled, and suddenly he slipped on the slimy wet floor.

He stumbled back, banging into Dr. Johnson, who fell back against the desk behind her, and there was a sick crunching sound as Carlos's foot broke through the papier-mâché volcano. Then he jumped forward, trying to get free and looking toward the ceiling and shouting: "Don't take me again!"

But his foot stayed stuck in the volcano, and the volcano caught under the corner of the table when he tried to jump again, and so Carlos slammed into the lab table, and with a wildly swinging arm, batted the half-full beaker of vinegar into the air.

All the while I just stood there, my brain going in slow motion, still for some reason thinking that there might be a way to keep giving our presentation. I watched the beaker flying right at me, feeling like I was drowning in the gasps and screams from the class as everybody jumped up to see what would happen.

Then Mr. Fissile grabbed my arm, yanking me

back, but my feet slipped in the slimy mess and I crashed to the floor. The beaker sailed over my head and smashed against the chalkboard. Glass and bloodred vinegar rained down on me. I barely got my hands over my face in time.

Lying on the floor, I figured that was it. Maybe one of the pieces of beaker had slit my wrists for me. There was no point in ever getting up anyway. I shivered as the clammy mixture of paint and vinegar drenched my back, my hair, and my legs.

"Trina, don't worry, you're okay," Mr. Fissile said from somewhere right above me. "Just don't move until I can get the glass off you."

I could feel him picking at my shirt and hair.

Now I felt a hot stinging at my eyes, and I figured that I must have gotten glass shards in them and at least I would never be able to see what a mess I had become — but it was just the mix of vinegar and my tears, suddenly bursting out of me in wicked sobs.

"Trina, wait —" Mr. Fissile tried to stop me.

But no, I was sitting up anyway. I threw my hands away from my eyes and saw the heads of all my classmates peering over the edge of the table. Were they feeling sorry for me or getting ready to feast on the kill? I squinted and looked away from them, hating them all.

I went to wipe my eyes on my sleeve but stopped when I saw the swirling watercolor of blood-brown and green that my shirt had become.

It was all still soaking into me, through my shirt and into my pants, and you just know that that is pretty much grosser than any feeling that science class should ever give you.

"Tri-ina —"

That was *his* voice. I looked up to find Carlos on his knees at my feet, his hair and head all bent up and to the left, his shirt wide open to his scrawny belly, his messy hands scratching like crazy, getting goo all over his skin, and his pants all soaked and red. His eyes were huge and white with shock.

"I — I'm so-orry I —"

*"Shut up and get away from me!"*

"Trina, relax," Mr. Fissile said, his face red. "You're all right, and Carlos — just — Marilyn —"

Dr. Johnson was bending down and taking Carlos by the arm. "Come on, Carlos, let's —"

"But i-it's no-ot my fault I —"

*"Yes it is, you little jerk!"* I screamed. *"How could you do this to me?!"*

"Trina," Mr. Fissile said sternly, like he wanted me to calm down, but I wasn't having it.

Carlos just stared at me as Dr. Johnson pulled him to his feet. "I —"

*"Shut up! I hate you! Get AWAY!"*

Carlos flopped like a fish, getting free from Dr. Johnson and falling back on his butt. Then he scooted toward the door and scrambled out of sight.

"Carlos!" Mr. Fissile called, but it was no use.

Dr. Johnson rushed out after him.

Ms. Atkinson was just walking back in. "Oh my — what happened?"

"Can you find Carlos?" Mr. Fissile asked her, still checking my shirt for any glass. "He ran out."

"Sure . . ." Ms. Atkinson disappeared after him.

You know, sitting there, soaked in paint and vinegar and the staring spotlights of all of my classmates, with a nice little cut on my left hand that was stinging like fire, all I could think about was what a total fool I was. Stupid, stupid Trina, who thought it would be different. Who thought that maybe Carlos was something more than what he really was —

A problem who ruined everything.

I looked up again, and there was Thea, and she was shaking her head back and forth, right there with me, on my side. Beside her, Donte was nodding his, and Frankie and Sara too. They all saw, all right, and finally — didn't I?

## CHAPTER 12
# The Long Drive North

That night was the longest night ever. It seemed like that vinegar smell would never come off. I was sitting in the bathroom, my mom brushing my hair after we had to undo all my braids and wash and now brush and rebraid again, when my dad came in and said:

"Listen, Trina, you need to try not to blame Carlos."

But I wasn't buying it. "He ruined my project."

"I talked to Mr. Fissile on the phone. The accident's not going to affect your grade."

"So?" I muttered. "I was up there covered in slime in front of the whole class!"

"I know," Dad said calmly, 'cause he could see I was beyond mad. "Just try to think about Carlos."

Like I'd stopped thinking about him and what he did.

By the next morning, it already felt like a week since the presentation. Time stretches out like that when you're so upset that you don't sleep all night.

Well, I guess I fell asleep at some point, cause my alarm woke me — and you know I had that feeling like my eyes had been taken out of my head while I slept, baked in the oven until they were dry and crispy, then popped back into their sockets. I got up and the first thing I did was repack the alien costumes, which I had kept under my bed — stupid me for thinking I wouldn't need them.

Dad drove me to school. Two long red passenger vans were sitting in the parking lot with piles of suitcases and sleeping bags in between. Everybody had these big suitcases with wheels, even though we were only going for one night. Ms. Atkinson and Mr. Fissile were standing between them with their twin clipboards and huge steel travel mugs. Through the tinted windows, I could see the heads in each van, and suddenly I just wished my dad would forbid me from going.

We pulled up behind, of all cars, Sara's mom's, just

as Sara was pulling herself out of the door. I huffed to myself.

"Still not getting along?" my dad said.

"She's changed," I muttered, watching her struggle with her bags.

"Of course she has," Dad said.

I looked over at him. "What do you mean, *'Of course she has'*?"

"Everybody changes at your age. You've known Sara for a long time. Now she can't do what she spent all her time doing. Think about what it feels like to be on the outside looking in."

"Believe me, I know how that feels. It doesn't mean she gets to act like she's been acting."

"But honey, sometimes that is what it means."

"Fine."

"Listen, go try to have fun, and talk to Sara." He leaned over and kissed my forehead.

And suddenly I was sad. Dad had tricked me into having one of those big gushing feelings inside, like I had this huge lake inside me and the anger dam that was holding it back was made out of tissue paper. So I hugged him and got out of there before it got any worse.

"I'll talk to your teachers again about yesterday before I leave," he said.

I walked over to the girls' van in slow, small steps.

"There goes another one. Tiger food!" Maurice suddenly called from his perch on the school steps, where he was waiting to be let in. "There goes another bear breakfast! Ha-ha!"

"Maurice!" Ms. Atkinson called. "That's enough."

I didn't even have the strength to deal with him. I just dragged my stuff over to the van and slipped into the second long seat, up against the window, not quite in total loser territory like the front row, where Sara ended up, but also not even close to the status seats in the back. Those were reserved for India, Latoya, and Kim Chi.

They were back there chewing gum, listening together to the tinny beat coming from Latoya's headphones and busting into rhymes together. They never bothered to make a peep during class, but a field trip van was their time to shine.

I slumped down in my seat, wedging my knees against the back of the seat in front of me and leaning my forehead against the window. Suddenly the seat squished down, and I looked over to find Thea scrunching in beside me.

"Hey, girl," she said, straightening out her pink sweat-suit top.

Before I could answer, Kim Chi called from the back: "Hey, Thea." I'd never heard one of them say hi to anyone else during school, even on a field trip.

"Hey," Thea said, and she was blushing when she turned back around.

"Yo," India called out, "we got a seat for you back here on the way back."

"Okay." Thea sounded surprised, but she was smiling too.

"Yeah, 'cause we know what's about to happen . . ." Latoya said. I turned back and saw them all nodding at the two of us.

I turned to Thea. "You told them?"

Thea shrugged. "It came up yesterday, after your tragedy. They wanted to get Carlos after school, but I told them to hold up, 'cause we had something planned. I bet you're glad we have that trick now."

"Yeah," I said, but I felt nothing.

Finally we were all loaded in, and two hours later, we finally escaped the Boston traffic. Pretty much everyone was asleep, except me. I felt too bad to sleep. When it was my turn to choose the music on the van ride, I handed Ms. Atkinson Heavyn's first solo album, *Strength in Number 1*. Here's what Heavyn has to say about feeling bad:

*When you're down, and no one's around,*
> *like a foreign clown, in the lost and found,*
> *Just think of me, and it'll be all right —*
*When you can't stop cryin', and you feel like*
> *dyin', and no one's replyin' so you wanna stop*
> *tryin',*
*Just think of me, and it'll be all right —*

And you know, today, even that wasn't enough to make me feel any better.

That drive turned out to be longer than anyone who's not thirty, or a senior citizen or whatever, should have to deal with. I leaned against the window and just stared out at the side of the highway passing by, all steamy in the morning haze. The cool feel of glass against the side of my face, the scrunched-up way that I was sitting in a ball, that oily feeling the van air was giving my skin . . . it all made sense with how I was feeling.

I watched the cars speeding by and tried to imagine who I might be if I was in one of them, instead of in here being me. I had already been a mom on her way to work in Boston, a young woman who wrote novels, driving to her favorite coffee shop, a girl named Jocelyn who had white parents and TV-blonde hair —

And on and on. My parents always get scared when they hear me talk about wishing I had a different life, because they think it means that I don't love my own. But it's like, how can you not sometimes just wish that everything about you was completely different, just to know what that felt like? It doesn't mean you don't love who you are, 'cause you only are who you are. It's just too bad you don't have a little card that you could use at, like, a store, to swap yourself into another body for a while, just until the heat of your own life cooled down.

"What's up?" Thea asked me later, when she was awake.

I tried to think of what to say about how I was feeling.

But Thea kept going. "I was thinking about tonight," she said. "Man, girl, I just want to say again — I'm sorry about yesterday."

"Thanks," I muttered, wondering: Was she really, or was this because of the trick?

"I know you were getting soft on Carlos," Thea went on. "I know he tricked you, making you think he might be normal and all."

"I can't believe he did that to me," was all I could say.

"Well," Thea sighed, "at least now you know we'll show him, right?"

"Yeah," I said, still feeling hollow, still feeling nothing. I gazed back out the window, looking for someone else to be.

It was another hour and a half up to Cardigan Mountain, and most of it was spent off the highway on these bumpy dirt roads through deep, wet woods that gave us all the sickness of a roller coaster without any of the excitement.

"I think I just saw a lion in there," I heard India say. Nobody dared tell her otherwise.

Except Sara, still *Queen Know-it-all*: "It might

have been a catamount. They're more likely to be found up this way."

I huffed.

Finally, we rounded a corner, crossed a wooden bridge that creaked like it might just snap, and pulled into a wide clearing. In front of us was a sandy parking lot. Up a slope of grass to the right was a four-story wooden building. It was white with long lines of windows and a single door on the ground level. Everybody groaned at the sight of the lodge, 'cause a resort hotel it was not.

On the other side of the parking lot from the lodge, a grassy hill dropped down to a tiny brown pond with a wooden raft floating in the middle. The pond had a ring of grass around it, and beyond that were endless trees. At the far end of the lot, a wide trail started up into the dark green.

We hopped out of the van and its smell of nacho-cheese chips, and the first thing you could notice was a different kind of hot, a different kind of air altogether. It was, like, cleaner than the city, but heavier too, richer and syrupy, with this sweet nature smell that was kind of like flowers, kind of like cut grass, and kind of like animals or something. And even though it was hot and all humid June, there were spaces in the air for this cool breeze to sneak through and make you feel fresh. That breeze must have been from the mountain, but you couldn't see it. Still, you knew it was up there, in charge of everything.

"Eeww, what is that *sound?*" Thea — scrunching up her face.

I heard it too: this high-pitched whining, kind of like humming power lines, somewhere up in the trees. But wait, there was also a buzzing that got louder and softer, like it was coming from a struggling old car off in the shadows beneath the trees — and this chirping, like car alarms when a thunderstorm was setting them off far down the street. Put all these sounds together, and suddenly this little spot out in the middle of nowhere was the loudest place on earth.

"All I'm sayin' is," muttered Donte, rubbing his eyes as he rounded the back of the boys' van, "those better not be bugs making all that noise."

"Oh my God!" Thea turned and started climbing back in the van. "I'm so out of here."

"You'd better get used to it." Ms. Atkinson — grinning like she had us right where she wanted us. "Just wait until we're in the woods with them." You could tell Ms. Atkinson — already in these big hiking boots with shiny buckles all over them, and nylon pants with the zipper-off legs, and this green fleece vest over her purple T-shirt — was getting some sick pleasure from torturing us like this.

Mr. Fissile didn't look much better. He was wearing this cowboy hat and a yellow T-shirt and then these shorts that had all these pockets and were, like, *short*, and let me just say: No kid should ever, *ever* have to see the hairy white legs of their science teacher.

We all got our bags and headed inside. The door to the lodge was on the basement level. Inside was a narrow hall with a million hooks for coats and things. A wooden staircase led up past a long dining room with a wide stone fireplace on the second floor, and up to the narrow third-floor hallway where the bunkrooms were.

I was maybe thirty seconds behind the first kids who'd come up, and you know it was already crazy up there. Donte was being chased by Thea because he had snatched her mp3 player, and Ms. Atkinson was trying to figure out who had turned all the showers on.

I took a top bunk. Sara limped in last and had to take the last bunk left, below mine. I walked by her without speaking.

Back outside at the picnic table, Mr. Fissile was passing out the rented hiking boots. Together with my mom's big wool socks, and my jean shorts and tank top and blue bandanna and backpack, I looked like a regular mountain freak. I was just glad everyone looked as silly as me.

We all lounged around, dark thighs, foreheads, beads, and hats shining in the white-hot sun that was burning through the steamy sky. If there had been other hikers around, you know they would have been shocked to see a bunch of city kids like us in this place.

"Ow! Damn —" Frankie slapped at his shoulder.

"Watch the language," Ms. Atkinson said, rubbing lotion into her arms. "I'll pass this bug repellent around. Please use your own if you brought it."

Perfect Sara pulled a pink bottle out of her backpack. I huffed.

"Okay, everyone," Ms. Atkinson said, "your backpacks should have only *useful* hiking equipment. No mp3 players."

We all groaned.

"Mr. Fissile and I will have *healthy* trail mix with us, and extra water. We're going to be out on a hike *all afternoon*, unless it rains."

"Shoot," Frankie mumbled, grimacing.

"Come on, rain," Thea muttered.

Now a tall guy with long brown hair and a beard walked up beside Ms. Atkinson. He was wearing a black-and-red flannel shirt and brown jeans, even though it was, like, a thousand degrees.

"This is PJ," Ms. Atkinson said. "He lives here at the lodge. He's hiked these trails hundreds of times and knows all about the environment here. He —"

She started going on and on about the wonders of this PJ guy, and when I looked around the group, I caught Caitlin's eyes. We both nodded to each other. Mr. Fissile had some competition here at the Cardigan Lodge.

"Howdy," PJ said, giving us a little salute.

"Hi," we all said back, sounding too hot and bored already, all of us, that is, except for Donte, who said "Howdy!" all loud and obnoxious.

"Anyway, so yeah, today you're going to be heading up into a very fragile ecosystem called the alpine zone. Have you guys all heard of that?"

Before we could even really mumble an answer, he said, "Right on," and kept talking. "Right on . . . So, the alpine zone —" He went on and on and Ms.

Atkinson watched him like she was so interested, and Mr. Fissile just had that jealous look in his eye like he was going to start challenging this guy's scientific knowledge with all kinds of superboring questions.

I was just starting to float away when suddenly, in the next pause, as none of us answered one of PJ's questions — I heard a sound that made my nerves shriek like a teapot.

*Scratch — scratch . . . Scratchscratch — scratch . . .*

Slowly, fighting the pain and anger that was freezing up my whole body, I looked down to the far corner of the table — to find Carlos looking right back at me, his right hand frozen in place. And can you believe that he even raised his eyebrows at me, like to say *Hello,* or *I'm sorry?*

Neither can I. So I just stared at him with no expression on my face. Like I was looking right through him. Suddenly I could feel the cold of paint and vinegar against my legs. I could hear the laughs and gasps of everyone who saw it happen —

All because of him. I just stared, my face like a stone. He turned away and started scratching again.

"Eeww, Tweedo!" Donte said, now hearing it too, interrupting Mr. Fissile, who was busy challenging

PJ to explain the geological formation of Cardigan Mountain or risk losing the love of Ms. Atkinson.

Carlos stopped scratching.

Donte looked at me, no smile on his face, and nodded slowly.

I nodded back.

# CHAPTER 13
# Everybody Knows

Two sweaty, sticky, mosquito-bitten hours later, we climbed over a long, low wall of rock and I found the perfect place to play our trick.

What is oh-so-annoying about anything related to school, and specifically Ms. Atkinson, is the fact that this spot was only, like, a twenty-minute hike up the trail — but oh no, there had to be *learning* along the way. And what was the point of hiking if you weren't going to get to the top? We spent, like, half an hour in the bug-infested woods, trying to use compasses and getting eaten alive. Finally, we split up from Mr. Fissile's "slow" group (not that Ms. Atkinson ever called it that, but you could tell 'cause it included Donte, Thea, and Carlos) and started actually hiking.

We wound up the trail, along a rocky river, then up steep slopes until we reached a ten-foot cliff wall. The trail turned and followed it for thirty feet or so, all the while with a sickening drop-off through the trees on the right. Then it turned and we slid into this crack in the rock that had steps carved into it. We climbed up, and at the top of the wall we were out of the trees and onto a wide, smooth rock ledge.

The mosquitoes and the black flies finally retreated, and we sat down for a snack. Even though I kept my frown on the outside, I have to admit I started smiling on the inside because it was beautiful up there. From this big open ledge, you could see all the way up to the summit off to the left, where there was a fire tower standing on top of a giant gray dome of rock. Beyond the summit there was the other shoulder of the mountain coming down across from us, with big patches of open rock like this one, and in between was a valley like a bowl. If you followed the fold in the middle of the valley, where the river was, you could see the lodge and our vans, and even Sara, a little white dot beside the penny-colored pond far below.

We were all sitting on the sloping gray granite, which started flat but got steeper and steeper until it fell into the tops of trees. Down below that was another table of rock that did the same thing. And back behind us, this ledge disappeared into a line of trees and shrubs, and you could see another ledge above us, and another, like these were huge steps for a giant to walk up.

And can't you imagine how amazing it felt, being up there? It was this cool mix of feelings. Luckily, we had our notebooks with us, and since Ms. Atkinson actually gave us some time to *free*-write, I made this list:

### COOL THINGS THAT YOU FEEL WHEN YOU'RE UP ON A MOUNTAIN:

1. Like you are finally as alone as you want to be all the time but never can be.

2. Like you are a queen looking down over a tiny land that you control.

3. Like you are a powerful and wise god, and the common people from down below should have to hike up here just to ask your advice about stuff.

4. Like — this one's hard to
   explain — like that you are so big
   that you are actually really small.
   'Cause up here the world looks
   tiny, but it feels *enormous*, and
   still you know that what you can
   see isn't even all of New
   Hampshire, never mind all of
   New England, America, North
   America, the planet Earth, the
   solar system, the Milky Way,
   the universe — like you are
   a giant and a speck at the
   same time.

5. And weirdest of all is this little
   voice inside your head that keeps
   telling you to jump. I mean, not
   because you're upset and want
   to, like, kill yourself or anything
   silly like that. It's more like, well,
   not even a voice, but a tiny twitch
   in your legs like they want to get
   you right up and run you full
   steam to the edge of this ledge
   and then jump you right off. And
   doing that would be no big deal,
   because obviously you could fly,
   and so you wouldn't fall. Instead

you would soar up and over the
trees and everything.

Do you know that feeling? It's strange. It makes me
wonder if there is a bird in me somewhere, like from
another life or something.

Yet these feelings kept being interrupted by another, a crabby one that reminded me about the day
before. And so that's when I realized that this ledge
was the perfect spot to take Carlos.

"Hey," I said to Frankie, who was sitting right next
to me munching on a candy bar that he had snuck
along in his bag. "This is definitely the place."

"Theh-play?"

"The place, for *you-know-what.*"

Frankie swallowed, then looked all around, making sure Ms. Atkinson wasn't nearby. "Oh, right," he
said, still looking everywhere but at me.

"See?" I said, pointing to the edge of the clearing.
"That tree there, and the other one over there —
perfect for a little flying saucer to go between,
right?"

"I guess," he said like he was half listening.

"Frankie, what's with you? Are you sure you're
still in?"

"Why are you asking me that?" He scowled and scooted away from me. "You're the one who was gonna quit on the plan."

"Maybe I thought about it, but so did you."

"No, me, I'm fine," Frankie said, and you know he said it a little too fast. "I just can't get in trouble is all." I knew that tone of voice. This was how I had sounded for weeks. But not anymore.

"You won't. It's a Thea plan, remember?"

"Yeah, you're right, I guess."

"Stop saying *'I guess.'*" Me — annoyed with him now.

"Hey, Trina." Suddenly Ms. Atkinson was standing beside me. My heart jumped 'cause I wondered if she heard what I'd been saying, but then she was like: "I'm sorry about what happened yesterday."

I just shrugged my eyebrows. "Fine."

"I know you're upset," Ms. Atkinson said. "I've asked Carlos to talk to you when he's ready."

I didn't say anything, hoping she would just walk away.

"Listen, Trina," Ms. Atkinson went on, and then I knew why she hadn't left yet, "sometimes when we feel mad, we think about getting back at people for what we think they did wrong . . . and while that sounds like it will make you feel better, it usually doesn't."

I was like: "Uh-huh," but inside my thoughts raced. I wondered: *How much did she know?*

"I just —" Ms. Atkinson said. "Is there anything going on that I should know about?"

I held my breath, turning halfway toward her, then offered her my best confused face. "No, what do you mean?"

"Well, please just know that you can come to me if there's anything going on that you don't feel right about, okay?"

Was this a trap? But I knew the teachers better. If they really knew about the trick, they'd have already talked to us all about it. Which meant that Ms. Atkinson had heard *something*, or suspected *something*, but she didn't *know* — and she wasn't going to.

"Sure," I said, then turned back to the view. I could feel Frankie being all nervous beside me.

Ms. Atkinson stood there for another couple seconds, then turned. "All right, group! Let's keep going!"

We headed across the ledge, into the trees behind it, where a small pyramid of stones marked the trail. We climbed through another crack and emerged on the next giant-step ledge. This one was narrower than the first, and not really flat at all, so we were all walking with a kind of a lean.

I watched the way the valley moved far below, and for just a second, I stopped. Caitlin and Shawn passed me, and so I was left alone. The voices of the kids faded, and I could hear only the wind, and, like, a distant nothing where there should have been the usual sounds of life, like cars and all. It reminded me of being on the ladder at Carlos's, and I had that feeling like if I stayed still for a second longer, I wouldn't be able to move. My stomach did a little nervous flip. I shook my head and ran to catch up with the group.

I found them huddled together in the middle of the ledge. Ms. Atkinson was pointing down at the bare rock. "See that? Veins of quartz crystal in the granite."

"Cool designs," Caitlin said, but I couldn't see over everybody's shoulders.

"Well," Ms. Atkinson said, looking up toward the tower, "we'd better keep moving. Those clouds look like they might have a thunderstorm in them somewhere."

The group moved on, and I stepped ahead and

that's when I saw it. The scraggly, diamond-white quartz veins made a bunch of interesting shapes, like crosses and all, but none were quite as interesting as off to the right, where the quartz made a shape I had seen before:

If there's one thing that is *not* annoying about Ms. Atkinson, it's that she loves to hike, and so, even though the afternoon was getting all dark and dangerous, she still ran us up to the top of the mountain. At the end, when we were getting close, she was a kid just like the rest of us, and it was all about how cool it was to reach the top.

Up there, it was almost too much, 'cause you could see out in all directions, and you were, like, as high as the bottoms of the big gray clouds that were sailing right at us from the west. Off in the distance you could see this one huge skyscraper of cloud, whose bottom was darkest of all. Definitely a thunderstorm, and definitely headed this way.

We climbed the fire tower in a hurry, and Ms. Atkinson took pictures of us all huddled on the metal tower stairs, including one with the little disposable camera that I brought. At the time I was so excited to think of having that picture for the last couple days of school. Little did I know then that I'd never get it developed.

We were just back down in the trees below the giant steps when the first thunder rumbled like drums above us. After that, it was only, like, a minute before the trees started hissing and we started just getting so wet. It felt so good to get soaked and goose-bumpy, to feel your feet squashing in your soaked socks, and to have all that toxic bug spray and salty sweat getting cleaned right off you.

And it rained all the way down, and then all the way until dinner, which was turkey and gravy and stuffing, and that's when it started:

I could feel it in my stomach. Excitement, nervousness, fear, guilt — it was all there and it was too much. I barely ate. Luckily, there at the far table was Thea's calm, nodding face, in charge, reminding me that what we were doing would be no trouble at all. Everybody else looked fine too — Sara all interested in a conversation with Mr. Fissile, Donte's face all bent into a big, stupid laugh as he wiped mashed potatoes off his nose, and Frankie, who was staring at —

Him, Carlos, who was down at the far end of my table, by himself — eating mashed potatoes with one hand, scratching with the other. God, I just wanted to throw something at him.

"Uh. Gross!" I said. I couldn't help it.

Shawn, sitting across from me, looked down too. "I know, right?" he said quietly.

"Yuck," I murmured back, nodding.

"It's a good thing he's going to get what he deserves."

I froze and looked over at Shawn, who instantly looked away. "What?" I whispered.

"At least you guys are going to get him good," he mumbled, still looking away.

I tried playing dumb one more time. "What are you talking about?"

"You know."

I had to fight myself not to raise my voice. "How did you find out?"

"Maurice was telling me about it yesterday, right after your presentation."

"*Maurice?* How did he know?"

"I don't know, Devon, I guess." Shawn kept eating.

"Huh." Did *everybody* know now? But of course they did, just like they always did. I should have expected it. Still, my stomach nearly climbed up into my throat. If everybody knew, then there was no way out of it — not without becoming the biggest loser in school. But then I reminded myself that I didn't WANT a way out. Nice Trina was dead on the science-class floor. This Trina was doing this trick. Still, I put down my fork 'cause you know I didn't feel like eating anymore.

"Good luck," Shawn then whispered. "We'll all be covering for you."

I was about to ask him what he knew when we all had to quiet down because PJ had started giving us directions about the longest and most complicated cleaning-up procedure you could ever imagine, involving huge buckets for every kind of food and plate and silverware that we used, and a tiny trash can that was only supposed to get your napkin, because everything else was reused somehow. Those buckets did not end up like poor PJ wanted. Mr. Fissile was probably happy about that.

We went back to our rooms for a half hour of reading time, which could just as easily have been called "anything-but-reading time," for all the reading that everyone did. Except, of course, for the one person who would be reading even if the whole lodge was burning down: Sara.

I stayed up in my bed, secretly moving the alien costumes and inflatable ship from my suitcase into my sleeping bag, and then into my backpack, and trying to figure out why it bothered me that *everyone* knew about our plan. I mean, Shawn was right, Carlos was going to get what he deserved, but it had been a long day now since the science presentation, and so the guilt-demon had dared to return. But I told it to just mind its own business, because I had made it happy once, and look how that had worked out. There was no way I was going to make the same mistake tonight.

I finished packing my backpack and looked out the window. Finally, it was dark.

# CHAPTER 14
# Sara and Me
# with the Bats

**M**s. Atkinson brought us all outside to play flash-light tag. The rain had stopped but left this fog that was so thick it was amazing. There was one big light on the front of the lodge, making a yellow circle around the doorway that stretched out to the vans. Below that, though, by the pond, the night was thick and black, moist and cool, and that's where we all headed.

In minutes we were spread out all around the pond, and it looked like there weren't any bodies anymore, only beams of white and yellow light bobbing up and down. They danced through the mist, which floated in patches like it was coming down the mountain in breaths from that giant at the top.

And you can imagine what it was like out there in the blindness, with a bunch of seventh graders. There was the running around. There was the hiding right at the edge of the trees, then the jumping out with a bloodcurdling scream. There was the throwing of rocks from unseen places to make hollow plunks in the still water, like a slimy creature might be raising its one-eyed head.

And then there was the *liking*. There were rumors in our class, changing almost every day, about who liked who, and who was dating and all that. And you know most of it was pretty dumb, because, like, what was dating in seventh grade other than talking? Talking about how you were going to meet on Friday night. Talking about how you were going to kiss, and then lying about how you kissed. Talking about getting sick of all that talking and finally breaking up.

*Liking*, on the other hand, was full of action. If you liked someone, you got to do all kinds of stuff, like deny that you liked that person, make fun of them at lunch, tackle them, and maybe even talk to them about how stupid dating was, even though that was what you were hoping to do with them.

So most of flashlight tag was actually *liking*, with kids tackling and bumping each other and sneaking away to talk about how they were getting sick of the person they were dating with the new person they were liking.

I wanted no part of all that tonight. I just wasn't feeling up to it. Sure, I liked someone, but you'll notice that I have never mentioned a single word about it throughout this whole story, and that's the way it's going to stay, thank you very much. Except that I did get in one good trip on him, not that I'm telling you who, although maybe you've guessed by now.

Anyway, I was walking around the near side of the lake when something zoomed past my head. At first, I thought somebody threw something, 'cause I heard a little splashing sound, but then it happened again. I stood still, turned my flashlight off, and waited. A breath of fog blew by me, leaving a layer of dew on my sweatshirt and jeans. I shivered — and then it zoomed by again. Only this time I heard the tiniest little whine and the softest little flapping of wings —

A bat. Now two bats, now three. Flapping all crazy,

like they were out of control, but really they knew exactly where they meant to go. They danced around in the inky night above me, taking turns diving down at the water like they were going to crash right into it and drown, but at the last second they would arc, like, inches from the surface and shoot back up.

You had to stare straight up to see them and kind of focus your eyes on the bluish darkness of the sky. If you kept your eyes still and stared at nothing, a little flipping dark thing would zoom by. You could follow it for a second or so before you lost it. Then you could pick them up again right down at the water, where they whooshed over the surface to grab mosquitoes.

I sat down in the grass. Four bats, now five. They came so close by my head that I wondered if they even knew I was there, but you know they did. They had me on their sonar.

Now I heard another set of footsteps slowly approaching.

"Cool, bats," Sara said from behind me.

"Ugh," I huffed under my breath. And you know that feeling when you are about to have to do something you don't want to do, even though a part of you has wanted to do it all along? That was me.

Sara sat down next to me. "So," she said, "all ready for tonight?"

"Duh, why wouldn't I be?"

"I'm just asking."

"Well, that's something new."

"What is?"

"You asking me about anything, or caring about anything I'm doing."

"Since when do *you* care about what's going on with me?"

I kept not looking at her. "I always do, I just haven't asked 'cause you'll just get all big-headed and tell me how I won't understand your *sooo* important life, like you did after the costume shop."

A bat swept down, like, right in front of our faces. We both leaned back really fast.

I thought she'd leave then, but she didn't. "So, I heard Donte's after India now," Sara said, then picked up a pebble and tossed it in the pond. It plunked far out in the water and, like, ten flashlight beams swooped toward it.

"Guess so. Whatever, like he has a chance with anyone."

"You know Thea likes him."

"She might like him, but she's not stupid enough to start *liking* him."

"Yeah, you're right." Sara threw another pebble. "Well, I'm sorry."

"Why are you apologizing about Thea and Donte? That's a stupid —"

"I meant for being a jerk to you."

"Oh." Now I almost looked at her, but then I kept my cool. "Well, you should be."

"And I am," she said. "And you should be too."

"Me?"

"Yeah, for saying all that stuff, about me thinking I was better than everyone, 'cause, like, you're my friend and you should know better than to think I would really think that."

"You're the one who said you had more important things to do than sit around Dorchester all summer, doing nothing like the rest of us."

"But —" Sara knew I had her there. "But Trina, I was just mad. That's not what I was really upset about, duh."

"I know, I know, you were upset about breaking your ankle and missing swimming."

"Yeah."

"Okay . . ." I sighed. "So I'm sorry too." And I finally caved in and looked over at her. We smiled, and a big wave of relief washed over me.

The bats were still circling around like crazy. One buzzed right by our faces. We laughed. Everything was fine, the two of us were having fun like re-best friends — then I realized that Sara wasn't actually laughing. She was sobbing, and, like, hugging herself.

"What's up?"

Sara didn't answer at first. Then she suddenly shouted, "I don't want to be so perfect all the time!" It came out all hoarse and choked up.

"Sara, geez, who ever said you have to be perfect —"

"They do! They always make me feel like I have to be perfect!"

"Who, the teachers and stuff?" but I should have known what she meant.

"My parents!" she sniffed. "God, I hate them!"

"Sara, don't hate them. They just love you and —"

"No, Trina! They're not like your parents. Your parents don't want you to be someone who's not even you!" She kept sobbing.

I searched my brain, trying to figure out what to

say. And what was so annoying about me was that everything that almost came out of my mouth sounded so corny. I didn't want to say anything like, *It'll be all right,* or *It's okay,* but when I finally said something, you know I didn't do much better: "Have you talked to them?" Some help I was.

"No I haven't talked to them!" Sara cried. "What am I going to say? I'd have to, like, win the Olympics before I could say anything and not sound stupid to them."

*"Mmm . . ."*

"Life sucks these days."

"Tell me about it," I said. "Remember yesterday?"

"Oh man, Trina. I felt so bad for you, you don't even know. That was the worst."

"I thought you were glad."

"No! I was sad, 'cause I could tell you thought it was going to go all right, and then Carlos went and acted like a big jerk."

"I hate him," I said.

"I know. I'm so sick of all of everything! So let's do something about it."

When I looked up at Sara this time, she had wiped her eyes and was giving me that look, the one that we always shared from across the Tubs, the one we gave each other when we just about knew everything.

I smiled back, and when the guilt-demon tried to grab my stomach, I squashed him. "You're right," I said. "Like tonight — who cares if we get in trouble? Who cares what our parents and teachers think?" I felt dangerous saying it, irresponsible, but it felt so good, especially when I reminded myself that being responsible was what got me covered in vinegar.

"Yeah," Sara said, flashing an even more mischievous smile.

Suddenly Ms. Atkinson's voice echoed through the fog. "Se-venth gra-de! Everyone needs to get up to the parking lot right now for capture the flag! Ten . . . nine . . ."

"Let's go do this trick," I said, standing and helping Sara up.

A flashlight beam fell on us.

"Hey, girls." It was Thea. Donte and Frankie stood with her. They stepped up and we all formed a circle. We were all friends again, no more problems — the Divine Divas on their *Add It Up to Number 1* Reunion Tour. The way it should be. Thea held the flashlight up, lighting her face like a sinister mask. "Ready?"

"Yup," we all answered.

"Everybody knows," I said, wondering why that was even still bothering me.

"Yeah, they do," Thea said, "and they'll all be watching." She smiled at me and didn't notice that Frankie turned half away from us and kicked a rock when she said that.

"This is going to be the biggest trick of all. Fame and fortune for the Tubs Gang."

That struck me as weird. I'd never thought of us as a gang before.

"Trina," Thea continued. "Go get the costumes and meet Sara on the trail. And on your way — Carlos is inside. You're the perfect one to convince him that he should come out and play."

I felt a flash of nerves. "But he knows I'm mad at —"

"You're the only one he trusts," Thea said, and the rest of the newly minted Tubs Gang nodded in agreement. "Now," Thea finished, "it's time."

Upstairs, I grabbed my overstuffed backpack. I grabbed my little camera too and shoved it in my sweatshirt pocket. I ran back downstairs and found Carlos sitting on a bench by the fireplace in the dining room, alone. His feet didn't even reach the floor. He was playing Pictionary against himself. While I was walking toward him, he flipped over the little hourglass and started drawing, his face only like an inch from the pad.

"Hey, Carlos," I said, as calmly and not-still-mad-at-him as I could. "What are you doing in here?"

"Hey," he squeaked, still scribbling. "Mr. Fissile's playing with me, but he had to go yell at Shawn." Now he looked up and saw my bag. "Sneaking off on a hike?"

"No!" I laughed nice and loud, and just for a second wondered if he knew.

"Oh sorry! I just — 'cause you have your bag and — oh, never mind."

I felt a rustle from the guilt-demon, but clenched my stomach against him. "You shouldn't be in here alone or you'll get in trouble. If Ms. Atkinson finds —"

"I'm sorry, Trina."

"— out that — what?" but I had heard him.

"I'm sorry. I mean, I'm really sorry about yesterday." Now he looked up at me with these big puppy-dog eyes.

Suddenly I was madder at him than ever. "You should be! You know, Carlos, you ruined our whole project —"

"I know."

"— and my nice clothes, in front of everybody, after I was *nice* to you and came to your house —"

"I know."

"— and I'm not even finished yet! So stop saying you know!" My nails were digging into my palm. "You don't know! You lied to me and you made me look like an idiot!"

"I'm sorry, I didn't want to make you look like an idiot, 'cause you're my only friend and —"

"Oh my God, Carlos!" I couldn't believe he just said that! "Don't even call me your friend, 'cause I'm not! And don't try and make me feel bad because you wanted to act like you do —"

"I couldn't help it."

"YES YOU COULD!"

"But I tried to show you my —"

I couldn't take anymore. "Just shut up! Forget it! You are not going to get me talking about your aliens again! We're not even going to talk again, period! Got it?"

"Roger." He sat there and stared down at his feet. "Trina?"

"What."

"Remember that time . . . you came up on the roof with me?"

"Do I remember it? Duh, it was, like, last week —"

"Thanks for doing that."

"Oh my God, Carlos, stop." I had to get out of there.

"Well —"

"Just . . . stop. Listen, Carlos, do you want to show me that you're sorry?"

"Whatever I can do —"

"Then," and as I said it, I felt something go all sour deep inside me, the guilt-demon's final try, but I ignored it. "Just come outside and play capture the flag like a normal kid."

"But —" he started, but I gave him *that look* and he didn't finish. He sighed. "Okay."

I turned, feeling something, like ashamed or just really tired, but that feeling was just more of the same old tricks. Listening to that feeling would just put me back in a puddle of vinegar, covered in glass, with all my friends against me. I started down the stairs, slowly, then I heard him behind me. I waited for a second at the door until he caught up. "By the way, Donte and Frankie were looking for you."

"Why?"

"I don't know, but if you're really sorry, you'll go find them."

"Oh, roger."

"Now. Go."

And so I sent Carlos off to his doom.

# CHAPTER 15
## The Trick

I headed out the door to the right, around the crowd and into the shadows. I cut across the wet, dewy grass beside the parking lot and stopped at the start of the trail. Looking back, I could see Carlos's little silhouette stepping cautiously into the fray of running and screaming kids and heard him call: "Hey, Donte!"

Right then, Mr. Fissile appeared in the doorway. He watched Carlos go into the crowd, but then started looking this way and that. I sank back into the shadows, wondering if he was looking for me. Then I saw him catch Ms. Atkinson's eye. She motioned to him, and he headed toward her. Swallowing a big gulp of nervous air, I turned and ducked into the woods.

"Sara!" I hissed over the whooping sounds of running kids.

"Over here!" she whispered back from somewhere in the pitch-blackness.

The little bit of foggy yellow from the parking lot ended, like, five feet onto the trail, and as I took those first steps toward Sara's voice, I couldn't see a thing. I was just starting to make out some blue shapes in the black when Sara grabbed my arm. Of course, for a second, I didn't think it was Sara at all. Nope, I was certain that it was a headless zombie or maybe —

Then she spoke: "Got everything?"

"Yeah."

"Where's the trail?"

"Over here. No flashlights till we get a little ways up."

"Right."

We started walking, and I swear, within, like, less than a minute, all the sounds of that wild capture-the-flag game were gone. There were only our two nervous breaths, and the crunch of three boots and one air brace on the rocky trail.

A little ways into those woods, I started to feel something different. Like, remember when I was saying that up on the rock ledge, I felt like I was really big but really small at the same time? Here it was again, only different — like I was a really small piece of something huge, so small that I could just get sucked up by all the black and silence around me and you'd never find me again.

But it also felt like Sara and I weren't alone out here in the dark, foggy forest. Like even the trees had eyes. Turning on my flashlight only made the feeling worse, because now there was this little spot of light to look at, and once your eyes got used to that brightness, the woods became even blacker, and if you tried to look into them, all you saw was the green shape of the flashlight beam that was still burned into your eyes.

And it was hot. I mean, it was cool, and foggy, but the air was really wet, and so I was all sweating and gross inside my sweatshirt and jeans before I knew it. And worse, I found out after, like, a minute that you couldn't even have your sleeves pushed up in here, because that was just like putting a big neon pink sign on your head that said *Free Dinner* for the mosquitoes.

It took us longer than I thought it should have to reach the fork in the trail. I started telling myself that we'd missed it, that we were done for. Finally, my

light found the damp wooden sign with its carved letters that you could barely read.

"Here it is," I said to Sara, trying to sound like I
hadn't been worried.

Once we turned left, we had to go even slower, and
the thick night got even deeper, and the sweat in my
clothes even slimier, especially underneath the backpack. The trail got all narrow, with roots reaching up
from the ground just trying to trip us. It wasn't long
before Sara was swearing under her breath.

"Are you all right?" I asked.

"I'm fine already," she said like her teeth were gritted together. "Just keep moving."

"But how's your ankle —"

"God, forget about my ankle! I — sorry. It hurts,
but it'll be fine."

"Okay." I told myself to shut up, because what
was annoying about me was how I sounded like I was
looking for excuses for why we should go down. If
Sara could handle this, then I should be able to handle it too.

But it just seemed to be getting darker and darker
around the flashlight beam, and it wasn't getting any
quieter. There were more creaky, sneaky noises out
there in the invisible forest, more creatures stalking

us, moving in for the kill. They would wait until we were tired, and then pounce.

One time last summer, when I was halfway up the ladder for the high diving board at the Parks Department pool, and I was freaking out about being so high, I started thinking about panic. Sara had seen how I was up there, and we made this list:

LEVELS OF PANIC:

Level 1: You have to pee, and then you pee, and then you already have to pee again.

Level 2: You have that cold, slimy sweat on your hands, and so you have to keep wiping them off, only one time, right before you're about to, somebody shakes your hand, and then makes a face 'cause that's *REALLY GROSS.*

Level 3: You start thinking about something totally random, like at the top of the diving board when I started thinking about that time that I was sitting at lunch

and the ice cream fell off my
cone and *into* my shirt, and how
everyone laughed and laughed,
and you hear that laughter in
your ears.

*Level 4:* You start wishing that you
were in your bed, home, right
now — and you start to cry — BUT
you're still able to move your body.

*Level 5:* That's it, frozen, sobbing,
call the fire department to get
you down.

"Three," I called out now, as I wobbled for a second on a log.

Then Sara said, "I think I'm starting to see my bed."

I smiled, just a little, then heard her laugh, just a little.

We kept climbing, higher and higher up the rocky trail, our legs burning. Suddenly my flashlight cracked against the rock wall.

"Okay, finally," I said to Sara. "We're close. Just stay next to the rock. It's a long drop."

"I wish you hadn't told me that."

We moved slowly. I was almost thinking of announcing level four when I started to notice a strange blue brightness above us. And then we reached the crack in the rock and climbed up onto the ledge.

It was amazing up there. The moon had come out, almost full and glowing softly in the hazy sky. The entire ledge was bathed in blue-silver, bright enough that the quartz veins sparkled like someone had sprinkled diamond dust across the granite — bright enough that Sara and I could see our own faint shadows. Around the moon was this huge ring, shimmering faintly like a rainbow.

"Whoa." I felt my panic drop all the way back to level one.

"That's a corona," Sara said, looking up. "It's — whoa."

I turned to where she was looking and that's when I saw that standing here on the ledge, we were above the mist and fog. It looked like a soft blanket pushed down into the folds of the mountain — this wispy gray-blue. It almost seemed like it was water — you know, like you could throw a stone into it. It looked like the world's artist had come along and just erased a big patch that he was planning to redraw later, and if you fell down there, you wouldn't stop falling. It made me shiver.

A cool breeze kept the mosquitoes away. I pushed up my sleeves with a sigh of relief. As I was doing that, I heard voices, and, for a second, thought the boys were already here with Carlos.

"Do you hear that?" I asked Sara, whispering even though there was no need.

"Yeah," she whispered back. "I think it's our class, way down there. You can see the glow of the lodge lights through the fog."

I followed her pointing down to the right, where you could see this little oval of light beneath the fog, with beams dancing around in it.

I could have just laid down on the rocks and soaked this place in for hours, but my nerves reminded me that we had work to do. I dropped my backpack and pulled out the costumes.

"Here." I handed one to Sara. "You start getting ready, and I'll put up the spaceship."

"Gotcha." She sat down on the rock and started slipping into the shimmery silver suit.

I blew up the inflatable saucer, then ran over to the tall tree at the back of the ledge. The ship came with two ropes, one for hanging it up and one for pulling it along. It wasn't until I was starting up the tree that I noticed the hard plastic case on the bottom of the saucer and remembered that it needed batteries to power its blinking lights. I swore, dropping to the ledge. Luckily, my flashlight batteries fit, except that meant that we were down to just Sara's light. But that would be fine. The moon was out, and Frankie and Donte would be here with their flashlights for the trip down.

I switched on the flying saucer, and red lights started blinking one after the other, going around it in circles. And blue lights blinked more slowly on the top and bottom. It looked pretty good.

I climbed back up and tied the rope as high as I could get. Then I dropped down, ran across the ledge, and climbed the far tree. When I pulled the rope tight, the spaceship raised high in the air, and settled up in the branches of the first tree.

I ran back to the high tree, where the spaceship was blinking and twisting in the breeze, grabbed the second rope hanging down from it, and laid that rope across the rock to where I was standing, right in the center of the ledge.

When I turned back, I saw not Sara but a Sara-sized alien in a silver suit with gold boots and about the biggest green head you had ever seen. "Watch this!" she called, flicking her flashlight on beneath her green rubber chin.

"That's so cool!" I hissed, then started slipping on my silver suit too. It was tight and made my pants bunch up all around my knees, and my sweatshirt practically choked me. Sara turned her back to me and I zipped her suit up. After she did mine, I put my backpack back on, and then slipped on the huge green rubber head.

The first thing I noticed was how stuffy it was inside that thing. You could barely hear anything outside of the big head because your own breathing and blood pumping seemed deafening. And I only had to take, like, four big breaths in there before the whole inside was coated with slimy condensation.

I turned toward Sara's big alien head, which I could barely see through the black mesh eyes. I realized now that the lights had been really bright in the costume shop, so neither of us had thought to wonder what would happen when we tried to see out of these things in the dark.

"It's nasty in here," I said.

"Wha?" I heard Sara say, sounding like she was a mile away.

"Huh?"

"I seh, wha?"

"Sara, I can't understand you!"

"Wha!?"

I ripped off the mask. "Duh! I can't understand you!" I hissed.

Sara pulled her mask off too. "Well, I can't understand you either!"

We glared at each other, then burst out laughing.

"So," she asked, taking off her rubber hand, switching on her flashlight, then putting the hand back on, "this is it. Of all the tricks ever done, we're about to top them all."

"We'll be the new queens of the school," I agreed, shivering again. That would be worth it, right?

"Famous in all the grades."

"Yeah."

Sara gave me our know-everything smile. I did my best to return it.

"And nothing," she said, breathing deep like she was finally free, "not even teachers or parents can stop us now."

"Nope," I answered.

And as if Mother Nature herself had heard us, the first big, puffy cloud raced across the sky and blocked out the moon for a moment. But Sara and I thought nothing of it, because just then, we heard voices coming up the trail.

Later on, after everything happened, here's what Donte said about getting Carlos up to the ledge:

"So we were in the middle of playing capture the flag, right, when suddenly out of nowhere, Tweedo was standing right beside me and Frankie. He was like, 'Hey, guys, Trina told me to find you.' And we tried to play it cool because Ms. Atkinson and Mr. Fissile both totally had their eyes on us.

"So right then, Thea, right, she just up and punched Caitlin right in the back, and Caitlin was all claws and everyone started screaming, 'Catfight!' and crowding around. And then Ms. Atkinson and Mr. Fissile dove in, and we grabbed Tweedo and headed for the trees.

"So we were dragging Carlos up the trail, right, and, like, he didn't get it at first, right, so he was still all like: 'Guys, Trina told me that you wanted to talk to me —' but by then you know I'd had enough so I was like: 'Shut up already, Tweedo,' and so then he started to get it.

"He was all: 'Where are we going, you guys?' and that's when I gave him the story. I was like: 'Yo, Tweedo, we need your help, Trina needs your help, okay? 'Cause when they were up on these ledges this afternoon, right, Trina and Frankie swear they saw lights like flying saucers, right, Frankie?' And Frankie was all like: 'I don't know, why you asking me?' and you know I just wanted to drop Carlos and give Frankie what he deserved 'cause you could tell he was all nervous and probably just thinking about his stupid basketball camp instead of what he should have been.

"But so I was like: 'Carlos, Trina said you knew all about aliens, and so she wants your help checking out what's up here,' and he didn't say anything for a minute, and then it was like something went off in that little freak, 'cause suddenly he started screaming loud enough to wake the dead! He was all like: 'No! You can't take me up there!' and he started kicking and bouncing around like a dog on a leash and shouting: *'They'll take me!'*

"So I just kept telling him to shut up or he *knew what would happen,* but that's when I should have known about Frankie, that traitor, 'cause he was like: 'I don't know, maybe we ought to take him down,

Donte,' and: ' 'Cause he might have, like, a heart attack or something —' but I was just like: 'Shut up, Frankie! You're not gonna wimp out on us now!'

"And so we got to the rock wall, and Carlos was all tripping and whining like a baby, and then he started mumbling, and I couldn't hear it all right, but he was like: 'This is it, this is the place, oh no, the place in my dreams —' but I just pushed him in front of me. And just before we got up onto the ledge and saw you, right, and all that happened, I turned around and was like: 'Hey, watch out for this root sticking out right here,' and that's when I noticed that Frankie was gone. . . ."

Sara and I could hear Carlos whining, so we threw our alien heads and hands back on, and Sara held her flashlight beneath her alien chin and I grabbed the rope.

"Hey," I hissed at Sara, "you never told me what you read that aliens usually say."

"Just follow my lead," she whispered back. "It'll be easy."

I squinted through the mesh eyes toward the edge of the ledge, at the darkness where the path came out.

It bothered me right then that I couldn't see so well, and I looked up at the moon and noticed that another, larger cloud was blocking it. I turned back to the trees, held my breath, and tried to reach out with my ears, but what I heard instead of voices was —

A low, distant rumble. It reminded me of how you could hear the subway at night sometimes, if there were no wind and no cars on our street. I turned to find Sara's big alien head looking back at me.

And then Carlos appeared. "Oh no, this is the place!" he shouted from the shadows at the edge of the ledge. The moon came out of the clouds again and we could see that Carlos was looking up at the sky, and, like, duh, he hadn't even noticed us yet.

In that last second before the trick, I felt my muscles twitching, like they wanted to send my hands up to rip off my mask. Suddenly Carlos looked too small again — Carlos who sat alone on roofs, not Carlos who ruined my clothes. I started to breathe faster. The inside of my mask got hotter and grosser. I wondered if maybe we should just —

But then he turned and saw us.

"Welcome, Carlos!" Sara shouted in her deepest voice. "We've been expecting you!"

Carlos stood frozen in place, Donte gripping his

shoulders. "Not you —" Carlos said, his voice shaking. I could see him tearing his shirt open and scratching like crazy as he stared at us.

"We have heard you trying to contact us!" Sara went on. There was a moment of silence. Sara turned to me and hissed: "Say something!"

"Um . . ." but suddenly I didn't know what to say, so instead I just pulled on the rope, and the blinking spaceship —

Didn't move. I tugged again, grunting as the rope pulled back against me.

"Come on!" Sara said, then turned back to Carlos. "There!" She pointed toward the stuck spaceship. "Our ship approaches!"

I pulled again, as hard as I could, panicking now. Suddenly there was a wicked snap and the saucer, pulley, rope, and the branch it was tied to came flying out of the tree.

"Aaaaah!" Carlos broke free of Donte and ran.

"Hey!" Donte lunged after him.

"Watch out!" I yelled, forgetting to use an alien voice.

Carlos sprinted right past us, and in the blur I could see him scratching at his head and heard a second of his hysterical mumbling:

"Here-this-is-it-they're-here-they're-here —"

And when I saw the look on his face, I felt this horrible shudder from the guilt-demon, and I understood something — I mean, I wanted to play a trick on Carlos, but I never realized that we were going to terrify him.

Then he was past me just like that, followed by Donte, but the free-flying spaceship hit Donte in the shoulder, knocking him right into me. The pulley came sailing right over him and slammed into my rubber head. Before I knew it, I was lying on the cool rock, pinned by Donte's pudgy body.

"Yuck! Get off me!" I squirmed under him like a trapped animal.

"Man, that thing sure didn't work!"

"Get off me, retard!"

"Okay, okay!" Donte rolled off and sat back, rubbing at his elbow.

I ripped the mask off and gulped in fresh, cool air. "Where'd he go?"

"Huh?"

"Carlos! Where is he?" I looked around, but I could barely move in my suit. Plus, even without the mask, I couldn't see so well because the moon was gone again. "He —"

And then I froze, as another deep rumble shook the air, the ledge itself, and all of my bones.

"Guys . . ." Sara — speaking quietly. "I remember what the moon ring usually means. . . ."

I scrambled to my feet and looked at her. She was standing with her mask off, looking up the giant steps toward the top of the mountain. You know, I already knew what I was going to see when I followed her gaze, and so I didn't want to, but like any horror movie, even when you know a scary moment is coming, you still uncover your eyes right at the last second, 'cause you just have to look.

The moonlight wasn't shining on the top of Cardigan — but it was shining on the slopes of the mountain *above* that, only that mountain was made of solid clouds.

"Whoa," Donte said, panting. "We gotta get down, now."

And like Mother Nature thought that was the first good idea she had heard out of us all night, a brilliant bolt of lightning sliced down out of the huge cloud, striking the fire tower, and making it shimmer a pale white. Thunder sounded again, only this time it didn't boom, it slammed its iron fists together.

233

"Where'd Carlos go?!" I looked all around the dark ledge, following the beam of Sara's flashlight as it swept the rock and the border of trees.

"Let's get out of here!" Donte shouted at us, edging back toward the trail.

"We can't go without him!" The wind just snatched my words. All around us, the trees began to sway.

"Carlos!" Sara hollered.

"CARLOS!" I screamed, my voice cracking.

Thunder tore the sky apart over Cardigan. It sounded so much closer than the last one. The wind gusted, and it smelled cold and wet. The aspen trees bent like they were trying to hide. Just like that, there was no more moonlight.

"Hey, come on!" Donte called over the wind, backing up to the edge of the ledge.

"Wait!" I shouted at Donte, because for a second I thought I heard something.

Now another gust of wind made me deaf, then faded, and there it was again. Was it sobbing, or more mumbling?

I turned to Sara. She nodded. "It sounds like he's up there!"

Then a huge bolt of lightning danced across the rolling clouds above us. Out of the corner of my eye I could see the veiny fingers of electricity spiking through the clouds. As the entire mountain was lit up like a camera flash went off, I saw a little silhouette on the next ledge up. Carlos was standing up there with his hands in the air —

Then it was dark again.

"Come on!" Donte screamed.

I turned to him. "Help Sara get down! I saw Carlos, I'll go get him!"

"Don't be stupid —"

But Donte didn't finish 'cause I was already running toward the trees, to climb up to the next ledge. I turned back and saw him and Sara heading for the crack in the rock.

The trees slapped at me as I ducked beneath them. Branches picked at my braids and my stupid silver suit. The wind howled. I could see the headlines now: *Prank Goes Wrong: Girl Found Dead on Mountaintop Dressed as Alien.*

The trail turned and hugged the rocks, and then I reached the next staircase. I ducked into it and was just popping my head up onto the next ledge when the first huge, I swear two-pound raindrop hit me right in the eye. Lightning flashed again, along with thunder that was so loud I thought it was the last thing I'd hear. In that flash, I tried to look around with my one eye that wasn't full of water, and for a second I saw Carlos. He was in the middle of the ledge, on his knees now, with his hands still up in the air. His hair was completely unbraided again and standing straight up.

"Carlos!" I screamed, then ducked my head back down below the ledge as an army of raindrops smacked me in the face.

Just like that, it was pouring, roaring rain. In the time it took me to take a big breath and wipe my eyes, water started to run down the stairs, spreading mud across the stone steps. For a second I thought of the rocky, root-twisted trail we'd hiked up, and I already knew it would be a mudslide on the way down.

I looked up again, shielding my eyes this time, but with the blur of rain added to the total blackness, I couldn't see a thing. So I screamed: "Carlos!" then ducked back down again and waited for the next moment of light. My back was already soaked through the silver costume, making my sweatshirt weigh, like, fifty pounds, and sending aching shivers up and down my spine. I could feel water running down all the way into my boots.

Lightning flashed again. I looked up.

Carlos was gone. I jumped up onto the ledge and stumbled forward, landing on my knees right where I swear he had just been.

"Carlos!"

"Trina! Hey, Trina!"

I looked down at the ledge below, wiping water and hot, salty sweat out of my eyes. That was Donte's voice, but I couldn't see him.

"What!?"

"Sara's —" But thunder exploded right over our heads.

*"What!?"*

"Sara's hurt!" I heard him clearly that time.

I turned back to the upper ledges. Carlos couldn't have gotten far. I started to get up, but suddenly I felt dizzy and dropped back to my knees. I started breathing even faster. Here on this slanted ledge, I was getting that nervous feeling like this afternoon, and like in the tree and even on the ladder at Carlos's, only now it was dark and stormy too. I felt like if I got up, I might fall right off the mountain. So I screamed into the dark: "Carlos! If you're out there, hide under the rocks until it's over!"

Lightning flashed again, and my whole body froze 'cause I was just certain this bolt was going to fry me whole. I swear I even felt the hairs on my arms stand up as the flash came and went. I looked down at the rock I was kneeling on, where Carlos had been kneeling just a minute ago, and saw that I was right on that circular pattern in the granite, drawn in quartz, the same as I'd seen on the drawings in Carlos's room, and on his roof.

I turned and scrambled back to the steps on my hands and knees, sliding down into the already deep puddles beneath the trees. I ducked back through the soaked and sagging branches and ran across the ledge, already shivering like crazy, with thunder and lightning exploding above me.

I looked back one more time as lightning lit up the mountain. I didn't see Carlos. So I turned and jumped into the crack leading down off the ledge and back into the woods. I nearly landed right on top of Sara and Donte, and had to jam my feet against the wall to keep from falling all over them.

"What happened?!" I shouted, my voice sounding wild now. Then I saw Sara's twisted face.

"She slipped coming down the steps!" Donte said.

"Donte, you jerk! I told you to help her!"

"I tried! She was holding my shoulder so we could

go faster but, like, the steps were all muddy and slippery and we couldn't see!"

"You should have been more careful!"

"You guys," Sara said, her voice all tight like she was hurting bad, "just help me to get under a tree or something, and then you get down the mountain and get help."

"Sara." I slid down the soaked rocks until I was right next to her. "Don't be stupid, we —" I had to stop as thunder shook the walls around us. "We're gonna stay together right at the bottom of the rocks here!" I shouted over the rain. "We're as safe as we can be —"

"Uh-uh —" Donte shouted. "We need to get down!"

"No, Donte! The trail is too muddy now anyway, you know it is." He didn't argue. "Come on, we have to get off this ledge before we get struck by lightning! Let's pick her up."

It took a minute to get Sara up, but then we finally dropped down the steps and into the trees. It wasn't any drier in there at all, but it felt safer.

"What happened to Carlos?" Sara asked as we all sat down, leaning our cold backs against the wet rock wall.

I had to wait to answer as thunder roared overhead. "I don't know," I panted, out of breath and shivering. "He must have found a hiding place. . . . He must have, I mean, I — I saw him for a second, then lost him."

"If he gets hurt," Sara said, "it will be our fault."

"Yeah, and it's our fault if *we* get hurt too," Donte muttered.

We all sat silent for a minute. It was easy to not say anything with all the sound around us: the roaring of the rain, the sloshing of flooding water mixed with dirt and leaves, running down the rocks — and the angry thunder drums. We huddled close together. I could feel Sara shivering and shuddering beside me, and I could almost feel Donte shivering through Sara. My teeth started to chatter.

I leaned my head on Sara's shoulder and could hear her teeth chattering too. The rock wall had become a waterfall, freezing my back.

"Five!" I shouted to Sara and started to cry. I couldn't help it.

"F-f-ive," she stuttered back and cried too.

# CHAPTER 16
# The Search

I don't know how long we sat there, ten minutes, a half hour —

Then we heard the voices. None of us spoke, 'cause we were way past talking at that point, but we all sat up at the sound.

Then we saw the lights, yellow beams, sweeping back and forth, freezing the million raindrops like taking a picture. The voices got louder.

Finally I shouted: "Hey!"

And the three flashlight beams found us.

"Trina!" It was Ms. Atkinson.

I tried to get up, but my cold, soaked legs wouldn't move.

The rain was still pouring down, but it had lost its teeth, and the thunder had slowly floated away. Now my legs told me they would try standing, only I slipped right back down in the mud.

"Don't move, all right?" It was PJ, the lodge caretaker, kneeling in front of us, dressed head to toe in a yellow rain suit.

Ms. Atkinson showed up right behind him in her purple raincoat and black rain pants, and then Mr. Fissile in his green raincoat and shorts.

"Sara hurt her leg again," Donte said weakly.

PJ knelt in front of Sara and flashed his light up and down her leg. Then he looked up at her. "Think you can hang on to my back on the way down?"

"O-kay," Sara said, chattering.

"Come on, you guys," Mr. Fissile said, looking at us like the criminals we were.

"Where's Carlos?" Ms. Atkinson asked, shining her flashlight through the murky dark.

I swallowed hard, and for a second, none of us spoke. You know, some stupid part of me was still wondering how much they knew and if there was a way to explain this so we didn't get in as much trouble.

"*Where is he!?*" Ms. Atkinson suddenly shouted furiously. She turned and shined her light at us. "God, forget about how much you're going to get in trouble, and worry about Carlos's safety!" I had never heard her that mad, and I never would again, but if you think I ever forgot it, you're crazy.

So I spoke: "He ran off up to the next ledge right before the storm started. I went after him, but I lost him, and then Sara's leg was hurt so I shouted for Carlos to hide somewhere but I don't know if he heard me and then I came back down and —" I was crying again now. The guilt-demon was taking over. I just couldn't believe these words were coming out of my own mouth. I had done this. This wasn't a story I was hearing about some other kids.

"Let's get down," PJ said. He turned so that Sara could wrap her arms around his neck. Then he stood up and hooked his arms under her knees. PJ turned to Ms. Atkinson. "I'll be back up as soon as we get them to the lodge."

"Right." She turned and disappeared into the crack in the wall. Over the endless rain I heard her yelling: "Carlos! *CARLOS!*"

PJ led us back to where the trail left the rock wall. We'd been right in imagining a muddy mess, but they had brought a thick yellow rope along and tied it to a couple trees along the way, one every twenty feet or so. We hung on with both hands, our feet sliding beneath us.

I wasn't even scared about doing this. So what if I died falling down this mountain now? If Ms. Atkinson didn't find Carlos, I would wish I had died.

All the way down, I thought about him, all alone and small. I didn't picture him up on the mountain, though. For some reason, as I grunted and slipped my way down the muddy slope, I kept seeing him sitting on the edge of his roof, so tiny, like the wind could push him right off. How could he be all right up there on that huge mountain? How could we have done this? I imagined his little body lying among the rocks, burned by lightning, broken and bloody from slipping and falling. I imagined Ms. Atkinson stumbling through a gray foggy morning, rounding a boulder to find poor Carlos facedown in a puddle.

I couldn't stop thinking of these things: the sad trip back, the funeral that I would have to watch from behind a tombstone on a nearby hill, and the trial in a juvenile court. Gray suits, prison food, a job at the local grocery store, and the guilt — no one speaking to me, my parents disowning me, a lonely death for Trina.

By the time we finally sloshed out of the woods and into the pool of foggy lodge light, it felt like we'd been gone all night.

"What time is it?" I asked meekly.

"Nine-thirty," Mr. Fissile replied.

Which meant I would be thinking those horrible thoughts for many more hours, for five as it turned out, until Ms. Atkinson and PJ finally returned.

After PJ brought Sara to her bunk, he radioed the local police and rescue units in the towns nearest to Cardigan. Then he took off back into the rainy darkness.

We weren't allowed to go back in the dining hall with the class yet. First Mr. Fissile had us change out of the wet alien costumes.

Sara just lay in her bunk and didn't say a word. I changed into my sweatpants and a raggedy brown sweater. As I peeled off my sweatshirt, my soaked and ruined camera fell to the floor. I didn't even pick it up.

I headed downstairs, my feet echoing on the creaky wooden steps, and I knew that everyone in that dining hall could hear me. As soon as I stepped through the door, I could feel every eye on me and I just wanted to shrink away. I walked to the corner and sat on the long bench right against the rain-spotted window.

All you could hear was the crackling of a little fire in the fireplace. That, and the light slapping of cards from the nearby table, where Thea was playing a game with India, Kim Chi, and Latoya. Everybody else was either sitting just staring off into space, or reading a book, or falling asleep on the couch.

I looked at Thea, and she was staring back at me with a kind of blank expression. Then she nodded and turned back to the game.

I realized then that Thea wasn't in trouble. That Mr. Fissile and Ms. Atkinson didn't know that she had been involved. Thinking back on the night, I suddenly realized that when it came to actually *doing* anything that could get you in trouble — she hadn't. Except talk about the trick with us. And there she was now, sitting with the friends she'd always wanted. She'd earned their respect with the trick, and with how she'd used us, and they were teaching her how to act like you didn't do anything wrong. And what did we get? We got all the blame, because we really *had* done the trick.

I glared at her, but when Thea looked up again, her gaze was blank and innocent like she wouldn't have any idea why I was so upset.

Outside, the night was suddenly lit by the rain-sparkled reflections of flashing lights. A fire truck rolled in. Over the next hour, another fire truck, then two police cars, then an ambulance and two yellow pickup trucks with orange lights arrived. None of them used their sirens. Teams of men gathered together, with ropes and backpacks full of gear, and headed off up the trail. I think I counted a total of twenty people heading up there, all with little radios squawking on their belts.

Finally, somebody spoke:

"I think I hear a helicopter," Frankie said, lying on a long bench by the fireplace.

Nobody replied. I hadn't really looked at Frankie yet. I didn't know what to say to him if we made eye contact, so I was avoiding it. I still felt mad at him. If he'd been there, maybe Carlos wouldn't have gotten away. Maybe we could have gotten Sara down before the trail was too muddy and she hurt her ankle again. Maybe nobody would be missing or in trouble right now.

Except didn't I know better? If it hadn't been for Frankie taking off and telling the teachers what we were up to, we might still be up there. The other thing I felt because of Frankie was ashamed. I think I was a little jealous that he had the guts to not go through with the trick. I had wanted to get out of it so many times, but in the end I didn't, and none of my reasons for doing it seemed any good now. The guilt-demon was letting me have it. I thought I'd known what I got for listening to it, but now I knew what I got if I didn't.

"Shut up, retard." It was Donte, almost a minute after Frankie spoke. He was sitting over by the fireplace, by himself in a wooden rocking chair. "Traitor."

"You shut up, Donte," Frankie said with a scowl on his face. "Man, like you haven't done enough wrong tonight. You oughta just keep quiet for once!"

"Me?!" Donte sat up now. "What about you? You're the one who ruined the trick! You sold us out with your big mouth, telling the teachers!"

"You'd still be up there if I didn't." Frankie was shaking his head now.

"Yeah, right! You could've helped like you were supposed to, but no, little Frankie has to be good for basketball camp. Little Frankie has to tell on his friends like some baby tattletale —"

"Man, shut up, Donte." It was India.

"What?" Donte stood up now, and turned toward the three girls and their new friend.

"I said shut up." India — shaking her head, but she wasn't getting up.

"You heard her." Thea — shaking her head right along.

"Why aren't you saying that to him?" Donte whined. He didn't dare take a step closer to India, but he pointed at Frankie. "He ruined your trick!"

"It wasn't our trick," India said, with Thea nodding. "And Frankie's right. You'd still be up there getting all struck by lightning if it wasn't for him."

A few others in the room *mmm*'d in agreement.

"Oh yeah, right!" Donte said, turning now to look at the rest of the room. "You all wanted us to play that trick. You all helped out! Everybody here's responsible!"

Thea laid down a card. "You're the one who took Carlos up there knowing there was a storm coming. You knew he has problems and gets all freaked out —"

"Euh! Oh my God! You're such a —"

But just then Mr. Fissile walked out of the kitchen. "That's enough," he said in a deadly serious voice.

I thought I might cry right there. Listening to everyone trying to get the blame off them. Listening to Thea abandoning us. Meanwhile, poor little Carlos was still up there somewhere.

Mr. Fissile turned back through the door.

"Traitor," Donte hissed at Frankie as he sat back down.

I couldn't take it anymore. I probably should have been letting Thea have it, but I hissed at Donte instead: "Shut up, Donte! I'm glad Frankie told on us! I wish I had done the same thing."

"Whatever!" Donte — making his face. "At least —"

"At least you should stop taking out your own problems on everybody else. You're just upset 'cause you're leaving!"

The other kids started to mumble to each other now, and Donte glared at me.

But I wasn't stopping there. "Don't even give me that look, Donte, 'cause you know I haven't told anyone until now, even though you've been a big jerk since you found out you got into St. Anthony's —"

"Shut UP, Trina!" Donte shouted, his face all red, and he even took a step toward me.

"Man, Donte, you're leaving?" Frankie was looking at him all surprised. "You got into St. Anthony's? Why didn't you say nothin'?"

"Yeah," Shawn asked from over by the window.

" 'Cause it's stupid is why, God —"

"That's why he's been so nasty lately," Thea said, nodding with her new friends.

Donte looked upset now like I'd never seen him. "Yeah, 'cause I'm sick and tired of all you!"

"Naw, it's 'cause you're sad about leaving," India said. "But you don't have to worry, Donte, 'cause nobody's gonna cry when you go."

"I SAID that's ENOUGH!" Mr. Fissile shouted through the door.

The room went silent again.

"Whatever," Donte muttered. He jumped up and stormed out of the room.

Everybody just got back to being quiet, then Mr. Fissile served hot chocolate. We all had some, and after that everyone started nodding and falling asleep right where they were sitting. I don't know how long it was before I fell asleep too, but I remember being one of the only ones up for a while, with my brain flying high and far away, back to Dorchester, so I could think about all the things that had led up to this, and how I'd been so stupid.

The next thing I knew I was opening my eyes and cringing at the bright light from the open kitchen door. I didn't remember lying down on the bench along the window, and so I rolled and almost fell right off it. I was just about to sit up when I heard the voices.

Quietly from the kitchen doorway, I heard Mr. Fissile saying: "No signs of him at all?"

"Nothing." That was Ms. Atkinson, and she sounded exhausted and hoarse from the search. "Except for some muddy footprints a few ledges up from where we found the others."

"Now what?"

"Well, the search teams will keep looking. They're moving onto the back side of the mountain."

"Maybe he got disoriented while he was up there, headed down the wrong way —"

"Dammit," Ms. Atkinson swore, "we *knew* they were up to something. . . ."

"I thought we had an eye on them."

"They had costumes and everything. . . . I mean, Trina? Sara? I —"

"Can't believe I left him alone in the dining room. Just to yell at Shawn about tripping people . . ." Mr. Fissile went on. "And they all knew about it, every single kid. I heard them talking. . . ."

Then they were silent. I heard someone sipping something, probably coffee.

"We need to start making the phone calls."

"The lists are in my bunk. I'm heading back out."

Their footsteps disappeared back into the kitchen. I squinted my eyes against the bright sliver of light from the doorway, and fresh tears.

# CHAPTER 17
## Questions

Sometime later, I opened my eyes again. It was still dark, the crack of light still coming from the kitchen. I sat up. Most of the kids had gone up to their beds. Shawn was snoring on the floor by the fire. I shook my head, still seeing this dream that felt so real — it was about Carlos and me. We were sitting on the edge of his roof, looking out at the Blue Hills, and I was explaining weather instruments to him, and it was so much like that real day that I totally thought we were back there and everything was fine. What's even weirder, and maybe this has happened to you too, was that my brain actually said to me in my dream: *Whew, it's a good thing we didn't actually play that trick yet where Carlos ends up lost. That would have been a nightmare. Well, now we don't have to do it.*

Of course, there were all these freaky weird things in the dream too, like headless plastic dolls walking around the roof. And, like, Carlos was covered in these tiny bugs, like those people you see covered in bees, only these were little aliens. You could tell because their little spaceships kept landing on his nose. And I'm not even going to start trying to explain how there were thunderstorms below us, clouds, lightning and all, and how you could dip your feet in the foamy tops of the clouds. . . .

The point is, when I finally woke up and my brain got its bearings, reality hit me like a giant balloon filled with freezing water. I tried closing my eyes one more time, to see if this was a dream that maybe I could wake up from. No luck. The nightmare was real.

Then a voice whispered to me: "Hey." I turned my head to find Sara sitting beside me, wrapped in a blanket and staring out into the darkness. Red lights were flashing on her face from the trucks outside. She looked all pale and had dark circles around her eyes.

"Hey."

"Storm's over for now."

"Did they find him yet?"

"I don't know."

"They've got to find him," I said, and started slipping on my soggy shoes. "Want to go down and see what's up?"

"I guess."

We walked slowly downstairs, Sara leaning on my shoulder, me feeling my way along the railing. The meeting room and hallway were silent and empty, so we headed out into the parking lot. Mr. Fissile was sitting on top of the picnic table, at the edge of the circle of light, both his hands around a mug. The fire engines, police cars, yellow pickups, and ambulance were all still there. He turned when our feet started crunching on the gravel.

"Hey, girls."

"Any news?" I asked him, not meeting his eyes.

"Not yet. Ms. Atkinson went back up two hours ago." Mr. Fissile looked at us for a minute, and the look on his face was so tired, but it was also so disappointed, I wanted to run. Then he turned away.

We just stood there. A big herd of fog blew by. The flashing truck lights reflected in the low clouds that were down below the treetops. Dripping sounds came from everywhere.

Now we heard voices. Three men in long rain-coats walked out of the dark trail and into the parking lot, flashlight beams swinging in front of them. They were soaked, their boots squishing in the mud and puddles. They walked to the back of one of the pickup trucks and threw their bags in like they were about to just fall asleep right there. Their radios started crackling, and one pulled his off his belt and talked back:

"Copy that. Simms, Jones, and Reynolds are down at base. We covered south slope and the red trail, no signs of him. We'll be back in at dawn, over."

The truck coughed to life, its headlights shooting into the fog over the edge of the hill. Sara and Mr. Fissile and I sat there watching the three pulling off all of their wet gear. I was afraid to make any sound. One guy, the tallest, with curly hair, climbed up into the back of the truck. He dug around for a minute and came up with a dirty old baseball cap. He stood up and was about to put it on when he stopped and shouted: "Hey!"

In the dark, it was hard to tell which way he was looking. My stomach cringed because I just figured he was going to yell at me, but now one of the others aimed a flashlight at him. He was looking the other way, over the vans and down toward the pond.

"Hey, kid!" he called. "Get back up here! We don't want to lose another one." He shined his own flashlight down toward the pond, then shouted again, "Hey, kid!" After another second he turned to us. "Sir," he said to Mr. Fissile, who was already getting up and walking toward the truck, "you should get that kid away from the pond."

"Sure," Mr. Fissile said, but his face was scrunched up like he was confused. He turned to Sara and me. "Did anyone else come down with you? I was sure everyone else was in bed."

"Maybe it's Donte," I said. "Maybe he snuck out another way."

"Well . . ." Mr. Fissile turned and walked toward the vans.

As he disappeared between them, the pickup truck started backing up, making this loud beeping sound with its taillights flashing at us in red. And so even though we heard Mr. Fissile calling to whatever kid was down there, we couldn't hear what he said.

And so Sara and I sat there for two more minutes, feeling two more minutes of fear and two more minutes of guilt and two more minutes of shame and then Mr. Fissile came back around the vans again, running, with his arm around —

Carlos.

It was all a blur. He rushed right past us. Carlos was staring at the ground through his soaking-wet hair. His clothes were a mess of mud. They disappeared through the lodge door.

I looked over at Sara, and she looked back at me, and we hugged and cried all over.

Morning came, and with it more gray and more rain.

I got a little more sleep after Carlos came back, but it was broken up by the sounds of boots clomping around downstairs.

Carlos was gone when we got up. Ms. Atkinson took him to the local hospital just to make sure he was all right, which, according to Mr. Fissile, he was, aside from being really cold and really scared and having a sprained ankle. And meanwhile we had to pack up and get ready to go right away. I didn't even see Carlos again until the last day of school.

But that doesn't mean I didn't hear about him

almost every second. The rumors and stories changed at least five times before we were even out of the vans from the pouring-rain ride home. By the last day of school, the story of what had happened to Carlos on our overnight to New Hampshire had become a legend that everybody still talks about and probably will keep talking about even after we've graduated and gone on to high school.

And it was stupid, because at breakfast before we left, Mr. Fissile had told us what actually happened: Carlos had hid in the rocks during the storm, then followed the yellow trail down the east side of the mountain. He told Mr. Fissile that you could see the yellow paint marks once the storm had passed, 'cause the moon came back out up on the mountain. But then he got down into the fog, and he got confused. The trail took him right to the pond, but in the fog he couldn't tell he was so close to the lodge, and his ankle hurt, so he decided to sit and wait for morning, and then those men saw him.

But none of that mattered to our class, and on that rainy, forever-long drive home, the legend started anyway:

India: "I heard that when Mr. Fissile found him his eyes were still glowing green."

Kim Chi: "And when he first tried to pick him up he got a shock so bad it burned all the hair on his arms and turned it black."

Latoya: "It already was black, only now it's curly."

Thea, who was now sitting in back: "That is so gross."

India: "I heard from Shawn that when Carlos came upstairs, right, he could only talk in these freaky clicking sounds."

Kim Chi: "Yeah, and Antonio said that when Frankie said hi to Carlos, he just looked back at him, and then Frankie started flipping out 'cause Carlos was reading his mind."

Latoya: "And did you see the marks on his wrists? They look like somebody tied him up."

Thea: "Shawn said he had bloody circles on his ankles too."

India: "Now how'd he see those unless he was watchin' Carlos change!"

"Uugh," they all said at once.

Kim Chi: "Plus, did you guys hear that when Mr. Fissile first called to Carlos, Carlos walked across the pond, like, without falling in?"

Latoya: "And, when Mr. Fissile brought him in, right, he was, like, totally dry."

Thea: "I heard from Donte that it was all a big hoax. He said Carlos was hiding underneath his bunk bed the whole time, just to get more attention."

India: "I'm sayin', right? The whole point of *that thing* was to get him to stop acting like such a freak to get attention all the time, but now he's getting even more. Listen to us talkin' nonstop about Tweedo."

"Nice goin', girls!" India shouted up at us.

I looked over at Sara. Her eyes were closed, so I thought maybe she hadn't heard what India just said to us, but then she slowly lifted her hand, made a fist with her middle finger up, and pushed it against the seat. I smiled, but only on the outside.

If the stories got even crazier between the time we got back and the end of the week, I didn't get to hear about it, and neither did Sara or Donte. We were all suspended the rest of the week. That's right — me, suspended. And Ms. Atkinson and Principal Davis said it would have been longer if school wasn't ending. Of course you know my parents were going to turn that suspension into a grounding that might go on all summer. So I spent four days walking downstairs, finding my dad at the table, and instead of having him tell me interesting facts, he would just shake his head, saying:

"*Mmm-hmm* . . . daughter of mine . . ." Of course he wasn't just shaking his head when he and Mom picked me up the afternoon we got home — he was way too busy slamming doors and being so mad, and saying things like: "I'm so disappointed in you."

And when I was like: "Dad, I —"

He was all: "No — WHAT made you think that some messy clothes and being embarrassed gave you the right to put that boy's life in danger?"

"Dad, I —"

"Don't try to talk to me now, girl. You could've been talking to me this whole time about all of this, but instead you went off and did what you did. . . ."

It was the longest weekend ever. And so, like I said, by the time I got to school on Monday, there was really only one story left about Carlos, and while it didn't have the walking-on-water part in it anymore, it did still have the part about the mind reading.

And what was most annoying about everyone, though, was that this final story didn't say anything about what had really happened to Carlos up on the mountain. It was like nobody cared. What were the rocks like that he hid in? Was he scared? What was it like up there, all alone?

And nobody cared how Carlos was doing afterward either. They didn't include his sprained ankle in the legend, or the cold he caught, or how he was out of school for the rest of the week too. And you know, they sure didn't include the fact that despite those things, otherwise Carlos was going to be all right, and that was, like, so lucky it was practically a miracle.

No, instead, it was all: Carlos the freak and how he'd been abducted by aliens. Guess that was easier than blaming the people who were really responsible.

So, then it was Monday, the last day of school, and everyone was tired and annoyed because school should never end on a Monday, but you know like four months ago, there had to be one too many snow days that everybody thought was the greatest thing at the time, but now seemed like torture. Half the kids didn't even show up, but you know my parents were making me come to school after what had happened. It was just a half day, but it was, like, a hundred degrees and way too sticky, and there was only one little fan buzzing in the window, and everyone smelled and there was nothing to do. Sara and I kept rolling our eyes at each other, like inmates in a prison waiting to break out, except that we were both still grounded, so it would have been breaking out from one prison to another. But we were also rolling our eyes because —

Carlos was late. The minutes were ticking by. Ms. Atkinson was trying to teach us the last fifty years of American history in one class, but she looked sunburned and exhausted and like she wanted to be anywhere else too. So she went on and on and we were all watching the door —

But Carlos came in looking normal, his hair in nice braids, wearing long baggy shorts and a blue-and-red-checkered shirt, 'cause kids who hadn't been suspended got to dress down on the last day of school. And he apologized in his normal voice and sat down and that was that.

For the rest of the day, I could only watch him, and listen to the new voice that had arrived in my head, the one that wouldn't stop asking all these questions.

During English — while he was doodling like he always did: *How's he doing? Did he see doctors? How's his ankle?*

And in art, while Carlos painted a tiny picture in the corner of his paper like he always did: *What did his mom say? Is he still sick?*

And at recess, when I was standing in the shade, with all the boys going back and forth in their football game, and watching little Carlos dig a stick into one of the long cracks in the pavement of the blurry hot parking lot, like he always did: *Did he see a mountain lion or anything?*

Every time I looked at him, all I could think was: *How is Carlos?* I just couldn't make the voice go away.

At the end of science class, Mr. Fissile had us cleaning the whole room. And you know that meant that Maurice was going to be diving onto the floor and seeing how many tiles he could slide across on his belly. And you know that meant India, Kim Chi, and Latoya were going to *not* clean anything, along with their new friend, Thea.

I was kneeling under the desk, sweeping dust and chocolate crumbs into a dustpan, when a triangle of paper bounced off my ear and onto the floor. I stopped for a second, unfolded the note, and read the three words on it:

Tubs. After school.

It was from Thea. The guilt-demon shook me again. I hadn't even talked to Thea since the trip. She had never gotten in trouble at all. Instead she'd gotten a new set of friends. Why did she want to see us? Was she going to bring her new friends along and have a ceremony to formally kick us out of the Tubs?

I didn't even want to go. But then I thought I would, just to see Donte for the last time before he switched schools, and Frankie before he went to camp, and maybe even to give Thea a piece of my mind.

I passed the note to Sara and had just started sweeping again when I heard all these loud noises, like gunshots in the tiny classroom. When I looked up, I saw Carlos, standing beside Mr. Fissile. He was dropping things onto the front table, then reaching into his pockets for more and dropping them too.

I stood up and I almost died when I saw what Carlos was doing. He was returning all of the microscope eyepieces that he'd stolen, and some magnifying glasses, and even a whole pair of binoculars. By the time he finished, there were, like, ten objects on the table.

"Um, thanks, I guess —" Mr. Fissile scratched his chin.

"I'm sorry I took them," Carlos said in his scratchy little voice.

"Well, Carlos, I guess I'm just glad you decided to bring them back and own up to it."

"Okay."

Mr. Fissile lowered his voice. "Good luck with your new plan, and have a nice summer."

"Roger." Carlos turned to walk away, but for one second he looked right at me, with no expression at all.

And so, just like that, school ended. Remember when I described how you waited all year for June just to have it send you along too fast? Well, this June had been like that too, except for the two endless days that I spent sweating at home, suspended. And by the time I had even gotten used to being back in school, I was right at the bottom of the steps and taking my first free breath of the wide-open, sour-smelling summer.

It's like your entire world screeches to a full stop, and suddenly you can hear the birds, and right in front of you and all around you stretching off in every direction, is summer. "A clean slate," my dad had called it as I was leaving for school that morning. It's the kind of feeling you just want to grab on to and hold — just keep that first breath in, to feel every inch of summer —

But Donte bumped me in the back. I let my breath out and turned around. "God, why do you have to do that?"

"Ha, yeah! I scared you. You looked as scared as when we were up on that ledge!"

"I think you must be thinking of how scared *you* looked," I said, but by the time I'd finished, Donte was already off and pushing somebody else like a big jerk. I guess that was the best he could do for saying good-bye to everyone.

I waited for another minute and Sara came out, with Ms. Atkinson carrying her totally stuffed backpack for her. She was back on crutches.

"Hey," I said, heading up the stairs and holding out my hands for the backpack. I tried to avoid Ms. Atkinson's eyes, but then she was talking:

"Girls, I hope you have a nice summer," she said seriously. "And we'll look forward to next year."

"Yeah," I said, nerves tingling, "once we get over what hap —"

Ms. Atkinson cut me off. "I hope you don't get over it, at least not anytime soon. I think you need to take your time reflecting on what happened."

"Okay." Ms. Atkinson turned to other kids. I helped Sara down the steps. "Why is your backpack so heavy?"

"It's reading for next year while I waste time on my stupid ankle."

I stuffed most of the books into my own empty bag. "Maybe I can help you."

"While we hang out doing Dorchester stuff," Sara said, and though she didn't sound super excited about that, she smiled and I smiled back.

"So," Sara said, "the Tubs, huh? This oughta be good."

"Yeah . . ." I was looking around the parking lot for something, and I didn't even really realize what it was until I saw it outside the fence, walking down the street.

"Listen." I turned back to Sara. "You go ahead, and I'll meet you there."

"Why aren't you coming right now?"

"Well, I — just tell them that I had to stay after — like I had to write another apology note or something."

We had had to write, like, a hundred while we were suspended.

"Okay, I guess."

"Thanks." Then I took off across the parking lot, out the gate, and turned left.

# CHAPTER 18
# From the Rooftop to the Future

I kept running, the humid air making my pants stick to my shins. Looking far ahead, I saw him turning the corner onto his street.

"Carlos!"

He didn't hear me.

When I got to his corner, I was totally out of breath. Carlos's street was as alive as ever. Tall muscular boys, their shirts off, skin all shiny, played football in the road. The music was coming from a different upstairs apartment, and this time it was a salsa, but it was still loud and seemed to be the beat of the whole street — the running feet, the double-Dutch game on the other sidewalk, the three wormy little kids with their huge squirt guns chasing each other around the cars. And it was so hot, and so loud, and so the first day of summer, that nobody noticed me.

Alexis was sitting out front, on the hood of a brown station wagon parked along the curb. She was holding Kasey in her lap and talking to two guys. They had on dirty, baggy jeans and sweatshirts even though it was, like, a hundred degrees. Kasey was chewing the head of a doll, like she always did.

The front door was open, so I walked in and headed upstairs, past the second floor shaking with bass, and up to Carlos's apartment. This door was open too.

Inside it was messy like always, and the TV was on even though nobody was watching it. I passed the kitchen and saw another pan of burned blackness, probably Carlos's latest creation —

And then suddenly someone stood up from behind the kitchen counter. I froze. She was short, like, even shorter than Alexis, but definitely older, with a bandanna keeping her dyed-red hair up, and warm brown skin and long red nails, and a navy blue T-shirt that said *6ᵗʰ Precinct Softball.*

"Hey there," Carlos's mom said to me. "Can I help you?"

"Oh, um, I — I'm looking for Carlos."

273

"Oh, well, now I don't know where he got off to. Try his room." She smiled, but then her smile faded. "And what's your name?"

I froze. "Oh —" Her eyes narrowed at me. "I'm Caitlin, from his class. He forgot his summer reading list and Ms. Atkinson sent me to drop it off."

She kept looking at me, and I knew she was trying to remember if Caitlin was one of the girls who had messed with her son. Then she shrugged and turned away. "All right, then."

"Thanks." I took off down the hall, catching my breath and trying to calm my nerves. When I turned the corner into Carlos's room, I had to step back out for a second just to make sure I had walked into the right one. There were still two beds, and a yellow beanbag, and that solar system rug and all, but it seemed a lot darker.

It was the walls, with their dark blue wallpaper, which I thought was new. Then I realized that it wasn't new. The wallpaper wasn't what was different. It was that all of Carlos's drawings were down and in a neat pile on his bed.

A stack of library books sat beside them, ready to be returned. I was glancing past them when the design on the top book caught my eye. It was the shape that

Carlos had drawn over and over and made on the roof — the shape from the quartz on Mount Cardigan. I leaned over the book, seeing that this cover was a photo of that exact rock. The title of the book was: *Nature or Visitors? Mysteries of the Granite State's Quartz Vein Symbols.*

I shook my head. Carlos and Sara could have had a nice talk about alien books. I flipped open the cover and ran my finger down the checkout card. A red stamp in the checkout column read: *May 24.* The day after Ms. Atkinson had announced the field trip to the class.

The window was open, so I walked over to it and that's when I noticed that the fish tank was empty now too. The top was off, and the doll heads were gone. There was still sand in there, but it had been brushed smooth.

I climbed out the window and up the ladder to the roof. There was Carlos, sitting in his spot. I made my way through the fallen antenna. There were still tons of bottles and cans and plastic food trays, but they weren't arranged in that circle-and-$x$ shape anymore. Now they were just scattered around.

I hopped up on the edge of the roof beside him. "Hey," I said, trying to be friendly, normal.

"Hey." Carlos didn't look at me. He just kept kicking his bare heels against the side of the house, making little slapping sounds.

I wasn't sure what to say next, so I looked around. The sunbather was out again, and there was a group of boys smoking, three rooftops away from us. When the hot wind gusted, you got a whiff of their cigarettes, and the brownish burn smell mixed in nicely with the street-griddle smell, and the sweating-body smell, and that faint salt smell of the harbor that made your nose twitch.

Carlos was gazing off at the Blue Hills, which could have been called the Invisible Hills today, because the white sunny haze was so thick that you could barely make out their silhouettes.

"You took your drawings down," I tried.

"Yeah."

"Why'd you do that?"

"They were ugly."

"I thought they were good."

"No you didn't."

"Well, but — I did." Carlos didn't say anything.

There was a wild scream from below us. I looked down to see this little girl running down the driveway between the two houses, with the squirt-gun boys right behind her. She was running as fast as her fat little legs would take her, but the boys were like a hunting pack. Just as she got to the back fence, they cornered her and totally soaked her.

I looked back over at Carlos, my heart pounding. It was time to say it. "Hey, I came to say I'm sorry about the trick."

"Okay." He still didn't look at me, but his eyebrows scrunched up.

"Yeah, so . . . I'm sorry."

"Roger."

"Come on, Carlos . . . I feel really bad about what happened."

"I know."

I kept going. "What we did wasn't fair and it was dangerous. And I wasn't going to do it! But then the thing happened in science, and I was really mad at you and, well . . . Do you accept my apology or what?"

"Okay."

"Do you really?" I didn't believe him. He just sat there, and what's annoying about me was that I kept talking. "Look, I know I sound like I'm only doing this because my parents are making me, but I'm not."

"Roger."

"Oh my God, Carlos! Can't you say anything else?"

He stared down at his feet, and his face clouded over. Then he said: "I couldn't help it."

"Couldn't help what?"

"What happened in science class. My problems. It wasn't my fault."

"You mean your *aliens*?" The guilt-demon yelled at me for saying that.

Carlos raised his eyebrows and sighed. "My doctor said not to call it that anymore."

"Your doctor?"

"At Children's Hospital." He still didn't look over at me. "They said that pretending it's aliens only — well, never mind."

"What?"

"Nothing. I'm just not supposed to. 'Cause it — it's not aliens."

"Did you *really* think it was?"

"Well, I — if it was aliens, then it wasn't my fault."

"What?"

"My problems."

"But they're not your fault even if they're not aliens."

"You thought they were. . . ."

"No, I —"

But Carlos kept going: "You played that trick on me 'cause I was so annoying, and" — he started to get choked up — "I thought you were . . ."

Tears started to fall, and you know I felt like each one was burning a hole in my stomach. I wanted to put my arm around him, but I didn't. I wanted to jump off the roof. I didn't do that either. So I just sat there.

Another minute passed by. Somebody cheered as they scored a touchdown out in the street, and somebody screamed a whole line of swears that echoed between the houses. All those curious questions kept stampeding around my brain. . . .

"Hey," I tried again. "So what did Mr. Fissile mean when he said you were on a new plan?"

"Nothing."

"Come on."

"It's nothing." His feet were kicking faster. "Just, the new doctor told us what to do."

"Who's us?"

"My mom and me. She said she should have taken me sooner, 'cause the school told her to but she was so busy."

"Oh."

"They did tests. I got some medication and stuff."

"Well, like, for what?"

"Well, for my allergic reactions, and some other things that I need to keep under control."

"You mean, like, to milk and stuff, like you told me?" I knew I was pressing him, but I couldn't help it. "But what other things?"

"Trina, it was weird, and I — I don't want to talk about it, okay?" His heels slapped the wall more quickly, like he was nervous.

So I backed off. "Okay."

We sat there for another minute. I felt like I was going crazy.

Finally, I said: "Hey, I'm glad you're all right after Cardigan. I was really worried about you while you were up there."

"Okay."

"I suppose you know everybody's telling crazy stories about how you were abducted by aliens."

"Yeah." Carlos didn't smile. "It's my fault for saying all that alien stuff all the time."

"So . . . Do you, um, want to talk about it? You know, like, about hiding in the rocks, or how you followed that trail, 'cause, God, Carlos — I mean . . . I knew you were scared. I — I tried to come find you."

"I don't know."

" 'Cause I could listen, or —"

"Nah."

"But, don't you want people to know the real story?"

"Well . . ." His face scrunched up. "I kinda want to — about the night, about the rain and the trails, and the doctors and stuff, I mean, talk about it, just —" Carlos's feet stopped kicking. He shrugged his shoulders and then finally looked over at me. He looked scared, or sad, or both.

"What?"

"Just — not with you, Trina. Okay?"

"I —" But you know I stopped right there, dead in my tracks. My heart sank down to the guilt-demon, who finally declared victory over all.

Carlos looked back out at the hazy hills.

"Fine," I said quietly. "I guess I'll go. I'll, um, see you in eighth grade, or something."

"Sorry, Trina."

"Don't be," I said. I had already hopped down off the edge of the roof when I turned back to find him looking at me. "I'm the one who should be sorry. See ya."

"Roger."

I climbed back down the ladder, catching one last

glimpse of little Carlos staring off at the hazy hills and feeling like my heart was shriveling up.

Then I headed for the Tubs.

I could hear their voices as I walked through the shade by the fence, but when I came out behind the warehouse, nobody was talking. They were all staring at me.

"Hey, guys," I said, dropping into my tub. I looked over at Thea. "Where are your *other* friends?"

"Who, them?" Thea — waving her hand at the air. "They got, um, other stuff they had to do."

*Plans that didn't involve you, Thea,* I thought, but then I hated that thought, because it was the same kind of bitter voice that I'd listened to about Carlos, that got me to do the trick that ruined everything. I fiddled around with my bag for a second and then looked up.

Everyone just kept staring. And they weren't smiling.

"Now what?" I said.

They kept looking. I kept looking back, and the more seconds passed, the madder I got. 'Cause it was because of them, my *friends*, that all this happened. It was because of *them* that I'd just been told I wasn't good enough to be Carlos's friend. So finally I was like: "Look —"

And that's when Donte laughed. And then Frankie. And then Thea. And then even Sara.

"WHAT?!"

"She totally went to Carlos's house." Donte — waving his hand at me like I was beyond help, and making a gross-lunch face like he always did.

"She adducted his alien like —" Frankie — getting cut off like he always did.

"Duh, it's AB-DUCTED!" Thea — correcting Frankie like she always did.

"Euh! It's AB-DUCTED!" Donte — mocking Thea like he always did.

"Wait!" Me — not wanting to joke about this anymore. "Listen, you guys . . . Carlos —" But then I stopped. "Forget it."

"Forget what?" Donte said, sitting up. "That you *love* Carlos and his little *aliens*?" He wrapped his arms around himself and started all kissing and licking the air.

"Oh my God, Donte, that's *REALLY GROSS*!" Sara yelled.

But Donte was way into it now, and he stood up to

get even *more* into it, and then slipped and fell right back into his tub.

Everybody laughed like crazy, and after a minute, so did I.

And nobody said anything else about me and Carlos. Not that summer, and not during the next year. I thought they would at least want to know what I had found out on my last visit, but they didn't. And you know, that only made me more sad. I just wanted one excuse to let everybody have it, about how we treated Carlos, but they never gave me one. It was like now that the trick was over, he didn't matter.

A train passed by all silver and shimmery, and as its rattling faded off into the distance, Thea said: "Well now," and she sat up in her tub like she was queen once more. Suddenly I felt my anger at her boiling up all over again.

"School may be over," Thea went on, "but come September first, you know we're going to have to do something to Shawn for what he said to Caitlin during recess today. . . ."

I sank down a bit in my tub, so that no one could see my stomach doing flips and my hands starting to shake. This was it. I was going to have to stand up to Thea. She'd gotten us all in so much trouble, made me lose Carlos, and now she was just going on like nothing had happened?

She was getting up on her knees now, still blabbing about whatever stupid thing had happened between Shawn and Caitlin — about to pretend that she was the smartest and the best like she always did, like we always let her, but not this time. I sat up too, and breathed in —

Then stopped. And even though I was finally ready to let her have it —

I didn't.

Why? Well, it was hard for me to understand right then, but suddenly I just knew something. I felt something in the air at the Tubs that first day of summer, and it kept me quiet as the group went on.

"We'll totally get Shawn good," Donte was saying even though he wasn't coming back. But nobody bothered to point that out to him. The way Donte wanted everyone to deal with him leaving was to just pretend he wasn't and to act like it was just another day.

"I'm sayin'," Frankie agreed.

Sara didn't say anything. She was reading again.

"*Mmm-hmm,*" Thea was saying, "the very first day of school, at lunch, we're going to . . ." She kept going on and on, towering over us in the warm summer shade. Finally she said, "So we're all agreed, right?"

And I was the first one to say, "Right," and then I sat back.

So, what was that feeling in the summer air, that afternoon at the Tubs? I figured it out later: It was the feeling that you get when you know you're doing something for the last time. Sometimes your brain knows too, and that's when the tears come and all that mess, but other times, like this one, your brain doesn't figure things out until way later. But your heart still knows.

As Thea went around the group, collecting "rights" for the trick on Shawn, I kind of had that feeling like I was back on the ledge at Cardigan, where I felt like I was so big I was actually small, only here, I felt so small in my tub that I almost felt big, like I was a part of all my friends. Suddenly it was like I *knew* what each of them was thinking, or at least I could read it off them pretty well, and I just knew that our futures were different, that this was our last time at the Tubs.

"Right," Donte said — but there would be no first day of school for him, not with us. Right then, he didn't know that he would make new friends in a St.

Anthony's summer program, new friends who had their own places like the Tubs. I heard one time from Shawn's brother Emanuel's friend Kinesha who knows a girl at St. Anthony's that Donte even tried out for the choir, and I guess he could actually sing like a girl and made it into the group.

"Right," Frankie said — but like I said, Frankie could *play*, and by the time he got back from Walker Camp, not only did he have *game* but I swear he grew, like, three inches and had all these muscles and on the first day of school all us girls were like, *Who's that fine new man?* And when we said hi to him and he spoke and it was still just Frankie, you know we totally lost it, laughing. Frankie started playing on the Boys Club team, and he had to pass all his classes to stay on it, so he was, like, seeing a tutor every afternoon and getting picked up by the Boys Club van right when school got out and there was no time for any of that stuff like worrying about what Shawn said to Caitlin. Frankie even got a little cocky about life, thinking he was all that because he could play ball, but you know we girls made sure to show him what was what, from time to time.

"Right," Sara said — but Sara ended up getting to go to Arizona even though she wasn't able to start swimming again until the middle of July. And when she got back to eighth grade, it was all about getting into the Latin High School, which had the city's best swim team, and so it was all about perfect grades and perfect attendance and perfect recommendations. Sara and I don't hang out much in eighth grade. She is always busy, and moving so fast, and looking like she has twenty things to do every minute and can only get nineteen of them done. We find time to make lists during lunch sometimes, or at boring old recess, but there aren't any more Saturdays at the library. Maybe when we're both at Latin, 'cause you know I got in too, I will write stories about her big swim meets for the school newspaper.

"Good," Thea said, and on the first day of school two months later she tripped Shawn on the stairs going down to art and they had it out, and they both got sent to the office and Thea got suspended. I guess that was enough to convince Thea's new friends that she was worthy, because after that, she was with India, Latoya, and Kim Chi most of the time. They played tricks, and bullied sixth graders for their desserts at lunch, and even started coming here, to the Tubs. But it didn't last, and Thea doesn't really seem to hang out with anyone these days. She's never asked me to play a trick in eighth grade, or even hang out, because I think inside, she knows how I feel.

Of course I didn't *really* know everyone's future while I was sitting there at the Tubs on that last day of school, but in my heart I knew that we would all grow apart. Like, what we had in common was changing, and was it a coincidence that it was just after the Carlos trick that we all started changing so fast?

As for me, even though I sat next to Carlos in eighth-grade art, and even though I would secretly get us to be partners from time to time, we would never really talk about much. He had some strange days in eighth grade, but nothing like the year before. No more Day Afters. Every now and then I tried to ask him about how he was doing or what was up or whatever, but he didn't really say. And it made me feel weird and sad because there was a time when he might have told me. That wasn't Thea's fault or Frankie's or Donte's. It was mine. And worse, no one else in school really talked to him, same as always. Even the jokes about his aliens were *so* over and done with by eighth grade.

But still I had that question-asking voice in my head:

*What kind of problems had Carlos really had? What could make his life so crazy that pretending aliens were visiting had been a better way to be? And how was it going now, when without the Day Afters, he got almost no attention from the other kids?*

*And what if I could have been the person that he shared all that with? The person who helped him out . . . His friend?*

But I wasn't going to get to know.

I'd missed some kind of chance with Carlos, and on the list of things that are the worst about life, missing chances will always be number one.

Thea and Donte and Frankie had moved on now. They were talking about all the movies they were going to see over the summer. Sara was reading again. I was sitting back in my tub and still having that shivery June, last-day-of-school, first-day-of-summer feeling of being so small I was big, like I could look down over everything and enjoy the view —

Of five bodies stretched out in bathtubs, in a circle like flower petals.

Of a silvery train catching the afternoon sun as it headed home.

Of a little figure sitting on top of one roof out of hundreds, kicking his heels against the side of the house and staring off into the summer shimmer.

Of distant hills wrapped in haze that always remind me of chances.

## Acknowledgments

There are so many people who deserve thanks for this book's existence, but none more than the two hundred or so students who navigated my messy classroom at Neighborhood House in Dorchester, learning science with lots of paint, dirt, clay (and without a sink), and the intrepid teachers and staff. Special thanks also to my family and friends for all their support and patience; George Nicholson for his wisdom and guidance; Alexandra Cooper for her help early on; Arthur Levine for making a home for Trina and Carlos; Daniel Handler for whatever he was thinking at the time; and Annie.